The Demon, The Dumbwaiter, and The Douchebag

Salvatore Cangemi

A HellBound Books Publishing LLC Book
Austin TX

**A HellBound Books LLC
Publication**
Copyright © 2020 by HellBound Books Publishing LLC
All Rights Reserved

Cover and art design by Alex Mcvey for
HellBound Books Publishing LLC

www.hellboundbookspublishing.com

DEDICATION:
For the three women in my life
Mom, for showing me life is too serious to take seriously
Judy, for telling me to "just write"
Catalina, for reminding me that magic is real

Demon: *noun*
a source or agent of evil, harm, distress, or ruin
 a supernatural being whose nature is to bring discord

Dumb wait·er: *noun*
a small elevator for carrying things between the floors of
a building.

Douchebag: *noun*
douche·bag

The term "douchebag" generally refers to a person with a certain combination of obnoxious characteristics related to attitude, social ineptitude, public behavior, or outward presentation.

Though the common douchebag thinks he is accepted by the people around him, most of his peers dislike him. He has an inflated sense of self-worth, compounded by a lack of social grace and self-awareness. He may behave inappropriately in public, yet is completely ignorant to how pathetic he appears to others.

He often talks about how cool, successful, and popular he is, yet never catches on to the fact that he comes across as a total loser.

Salvatore Cangemi

Prologue

1979

It was a hot and sunny day in August when the tree began sprouting money. The girl watched from her room window. Her father ran around in a frenzy, pulling bills off the old crab-apple tree and stuffing them into his Bermuda shorts.

"It's a miracle! A fucking miracle!" Her father shouted.

"Stop cursing," her mother admonished.

"An *effin* miracle!" Her dad corrected, slapping her mother playfully on the ass.

"Thank you, Jesus," her mother said, crossing herself.

The girl thought 'miracle' may not be the precise word to describe the oddity, and knew Jesus had nothing to do with it. But the money was real. And they needed it. Badly.

Her father had been unemployed for almost six months now. They were going to lose everything. And even though she was only ten years old, she knew how much the family's money issues were affecting their lives. Her parents were fighting all the time now. And so, she had asked the entity for money. She knew it was a bad idea, as the little imp had brought nothing but misfortune to her and everyone in the Le Trou Du Cul apartment complex. So many peculiar things were happening since the demon's appearance that many of the complex's residents mistook it for a haunting. Tenants were reporting coming home to find all the contents of their cupboards switched around, or finding clothes rearranged in closets. One woman—who lived alone—claimed that every time she left the apartment, she came home to a large "log" shit in her toilet.

As for the little girl, many of her toys had become possessed over the last week. Her favorite teddy bear farted constantly and stunk up her room so badly she would gag. A gross fish smell emitted from her Holly Hobby oven, despite it not even being plugged in. And no matter what 45 record she put on her portable turntable, the only song that played was *Funky Town*. She even noticed that the little figures she'd created in her diorama (a school project) would be in different places than she'd left them—as if they moved on their own accord. But what could she do? The family was broke. And so last night she called for the thing.

Her better judgment warned against what she was about to do. She had seen the trouble the fuzzy demon had caused. But she opened the dumbwaiter and summoned the fiend and made her wish.

And the imp, in his friendly/cartoon voice had said, "*moneyleaf*" and rubbed his little pink hands together, creating a cloud of sparkles. And just like that, they awoke in the morning to a this. And the demon and the little girl had conspired to prove her father wrong—despite the old man's constant saying to the contrary, money *did* grow on trees.

ONE

Le Trou Du Cul

The sound of laughter drifted up from the courtyard below, making him feel very alone in this new place. He'd moved into the Le Trou Du Cul apartment complex only three days ago. The place had a tennis court (he didn't play), a game room with all manner of board games (he didn't like games) and even a small "community" theatre where the members of the complex could put on plays (he wasn't interested). But he needed to be away from his old town, needed to be anonymous for a while. Le Trou Du Cul, while not exactly cheap, had an opening, was in his price range, and close enough to his job. It was surrounded with woods where kids could play and explore, but whenever Jarvis looked out his window, the few kids who lived here were staring, hypnotized, into their phones. At least they were outside.

He watched from his window as he cleaned this morning's breakfast dishes. The group of adults below laughed and drank beer. They were playing some kind of bean bag game and having a ball. Kyle Jarvis was happy to be alone. The day had been mind-numbing, and he just wanted to eat and go to bed early.

He'd only met a few of the other residents, mostly people on the same floor as he (the 4th floor). There was the Horn family. Liz was the mother and while nice enough, always appeared to be in a big rush. She looked as if she had once been pretty but now had some extra pounds and was always dressed in jeans and a T-shirt, with her mousy hair in a limp ponytail. Her husband, Buddy, and son, Timmy were large and small versions of the same model. Both fat and ruddy-faced with a smirk that made you feel that you had just missed a joke at your expense.

They had been the first people he'd met when he'd moved in. Pulling up in the lot in his rental truck, Buddy had asked where he had come from and how long the commute had taken.

Buddy cut him off as he'd been replying, shouting, "Christ! What route did you take, the slow-poke turnpike?"

Timmy laughed with his old man.

"Yea, a slow poke."

Kyle Jarvis tried to smile. Liz introduced herself and the family. Buddy shook his hand and applied too much pressure; held on too long.

"I'm Kyle Jarvis. Everyone calls me Jarvis."

"You like football, Jarvis?" Buddy asked.

"Sorry, not my thing," Jarvis replied.

"Not your thing! Are you kidding? You're an American, right? You're a *man*, no? How could football not be 'your thing'?"

"Buddy, leave him alone. He's not even moved in yet. You'll have plenty of time to annoy him soon enough." Liz rolled her eyes at Kyle.

"You need to get into football. We're practically gonna be roommates, you prick!" Buddy gave him a punch in the arm. It hurt but Jarvis resisted rubbing the spot. Timmy cackled and repeated his father.

"Yea, you prick!" The fat boy shrieked.

"Timmy! Watch your mouth. Nice, Buddy!"

"What, babe? He's eleven. He knows what a prick is. Hell, I was shakin' mine at nine for Christ's sake."

"TMI," Liz said but appeared to think it was cute.

"I played ball in high school. Varsity. No joke. I was so good that the teachers passed me, and I hardly went to classes. The girls lined up to meet me. I know I'm a fat fuck now but back then I laid more pipe in this town than Pete the Plumber."

"Buddy!" Liz said. Then more to herself: "Jesus."

"What, babe? You should be happy to be married to an athlete."

"Luck…right," she groaned.

"This little bastard is gonna play ball, too. But he needs to drop some weight," Buddy rubbed Timmy's red crew-cut.

"You're fatter than me!" Timmy cried.

"Yea, but I'm not trying to make the team, you lazy prick."

"Buddy?!" Liz shrilled.

"What? You know how lazy this son-of-a-bitch-and-bastard is?" He asked, nudging Jarvis.

"Uh..."

"He had a job delivering the penny savers to our building. Just *our* building, mind you. No bike required. I drove him to pick them up. Then he bags them. Then delivers them. What could be easier? Well he does it once or twice. Then he just gathers them all up, and then takes the whole lot out into the woods here and dumps them out there. After a few months someone in the building snitched—and I'd like to know who...I'd bust his hump. But the supervisor goes back there, and it looks like a bonfire is getting ready to go. A huge pile of these papers!"

He rubbed his son's head again.

"Nice, right?" Liz said.

"Little bastard is smart; can't take it away from him."

"Yea, so smart he had the job two months and got himself fired. A real genius," Liz said.

"See, babe, you never look at the positive. The way *I* see it is he got *paid* for two months for doing nothing."

"Wonderful."

"Well, nice meeting you guys," Jarvis said, itching to get away. "I need to start moving in."

Now as he looked out at the gang playing the game, he felt lonely. Yet he had no desire to join them either. Buddy was handing a beanbag to an obese man. Jarvis thought he'd heard Buddy call the huge man 'Louis' but was not sure. A number of other people were down there as well. A few yards off, a number of people were sitting around the man-made lake in the courtyard. One old man was standing at the edge of the woods and taking pictures. A bubble rose from the dishes he was doing and tickled his nose. He sneezed loudly. Buddy Horn looked up and saw him at the window.

"Get down here and join us, Jarvis!" Buddy yelled up.

"No thanks, I'm busy. Thank you."

"Shit. Get down here so I can corn hole you at corn hole!"
Everyone laughed.

"No thanks."

"You fuckin' pansy, c'mon!"

"Next time, Buddy."

"Ahhhh. Fuck ya, then!" He yelled, smiling.

Buddy did not seem like a bad guy, per se. But he was not Jarvis's kind of guy. He was a bit of a douchebag. Truth be told, they were both douchebags but different kinds of douchebags.

After the dishes, he busied himself with cooking dinner: stir-fry and rice. As he put the chicken trimmings in the garbage, he decided to bring the bag out to the dumpster. Luckily, it was in the back of the building and the corn hole players where in the courtyard with the tables and benches. He made his way down the hall but just as he was getting to the stairs, Marlene Davis spotted him. Ms. Davis was old.

Very old. She had been an actress sometime before electricity'd been invented and never made it anywhere. Her short hair was died an unnatural black. All the makeup she wore enhanced her many wrinkles rather than hid them. She wore a long black evening dress everyday, even though she never left the apartment complex.

"Mr. Jarvis! Kyle!"

"Hello, Ms. Davis."

"Marlene, I told you. Marlene. Ms. Davis is my mother."

Jarvis thought Marlene's mother had been buried sometime before the renascence.

"Yes, Marlene, sorry."

"It's a stage name, you know."

"Sorry?"

"Marlene Davis. It's a stage name. My *professional* name."

"Oh...."

"I was compared to Sharon Tate back in the sixties. Of course, I am more of an actress than *she* ever was, but because of Helter Skelter, she was immortalized. God rest her soul. Of course, I knew Sharon very well. I knew everyone back then."

"Wow. Were you in many movies?"

"Yes! Well almost. I was cast in a number of movies, my dear. But the other actresses were always jealous of me. They were usually sleeping with the producers or directors and I refused to do that. So, I lost my roles."

"Oh, I see."

"I was in a theatre company and I was supposed to be the next big name; the next leading lady. But another actress, Claudia Connor, slept with *all* the money-men. She also dated Pablo Picasso, so she got the lead roles. Then she died most tragically—she was murdered—and I was next in line. But I still refused to sleep around. So, it did not work out."

"Oh..."

"Have you met many people here, yet?"

"Only you and the Horn Family so far," he replied.

"Ugh."

"You know them?"

"Yes. Watch out for that Timmy. He's a bad kid—a real rotten apple."

"Really?"

"Really. I had to report him for not delivering the penny saver. Louis Green was in the woods, searching for Bigfoot, and he told me about the mountain of penny savers and I went to look, and I reported the punk."

"Well, you may want to keep it to yourself that you were the one who called the supervisor. I think Buddy is looking for who the snitch is."

"Oh, I'm not telling a soul. That family is crazy. And I would hate to rope Louis in as he was only doing his daily search and just happen to stumble upon it."

"Searching for Bigfoot you said?"

"Yes. He's convinced Bigfoot lives in these woods."

"But the woods here are only about 400 yards."

"There have been a few sightings."

"Oh..."

"Have you met Louis?"

"Not sure. Is he the heavy-set guy?"

"'Heavy-set'? Oh dear, you're a better person than I. He's the fattest man I have ever seen. And he works in food, you know?"

"Oh really? A chef?"

"Yes…well no. He's not a chef. He's a scientist. He makes additives for junk food. He's in the department that makes new flavors. Gives that crap all over the complex. Flavors that did not pass. Sardine flavored cheese curls, chocolate and garlic crackers, low carb pretzels made from turnips. Horrible stuff.

"Sounds awful."

"I'm looking to get back into the business, you know."

"I'm sorry?"

"The *acting* business!"

"Oh, I think that's a fine idea," Jarvis said, thinking nothing of the kind.

"I've created a one woman show. It will be performed in our little theater. A much smaller venue than I am used to performing, of course. But I need to do it to test the waters for my comeback. You will be receiving an invitation shortly."

"I look forward to it," he lied.

"I hope all the people in Le Trou Du Cul know what an honor it is. A chance to see a real star in such an intimate setting."

"I'm sure they do."

"Only thing is I suffer from some brain fog these days. Makes remembering lines difficult. And I have a bad hip as well, needs to be replaced. But actors do not get medical, you see." the old woman droned on in a stage actresses' voice.

"You know what will fix that right up. Warm water with lemon and organic honey!" A woman's voice said.

She appeared from the end of the hall.

"Fix what, my dear? The brain fog or my bum hip?" Marlene asked.

"Both," the thin woman said, coughing.

Marlene introduced Jarvis to Summer. She was a waif of a thing. A neo-hippy new age asshole. A white woman with dreadlocks. She smelled of patchouli and bullshit.

"So, wait. Are you saying that drinking warm water with lemon and honey will fix a hip that needs replacing?"

"*Organic* honey. Has to be organic. It cures cancer, too."

"That's nuts. If the hip had been worn down and needs replacing, how can that help?"

"Oh, you are just what the Western doctors want," Summer said to Jarvis, not even attempting to hide her disdain. She turned to Marlene.

"Listen to me, Marlene, don't trust your doctor. You're just a customer to him."

"*Her*," Marlene corrected.

"Huh?"

"My doctor—the doctor recommended the hip replacement, is a her. A woman."

"Oh. Wow. It's surprising that a woman doctor would recommend something so underhanded."

"But you just said Western doctors only see us as customers," Jarvis said.

"Yes. It's true. Western *male* doctors," Summer corrected herself. She coughed again.

"Oh, dear, you should try some of that honey and lemon for that cough," Marlene said.

"It's not really a cough," Summer replied.

"It's not? It sure sounds like a cough," Jarvis said.

"Well I am coughing, but I don't *have* a cough. Anyway, I have some herbs that I need to mix with the day's first urine."

"What?! And you *drink* that?" Marlene asked, appalled.

"Of course. It will fix me right up. But I have to wait until the morning to make it, of course."

"Drinking piss? That's nuts," Jarvis said.

"Really? More nuts than letting doctors poison me?"

"Who told you this is going to work?"

"A witch I know."

"Oh, well if the witch said so than believe her over a doctor," Jarvis said.

"*Him*," Summer said.

"Sorry?"

"The witch, who recommended the mixture, is a man."

"Oh…." Jarvis said.

"You really think you know all the answers, huh?" Summer asked.

"Well I need to get this into the dumpster," Jarvis said, holding up the garbage bag. "Nice meeting you, Summer," he said with a smirk and began making his way to the stairs.

"What kind of garbage is that? Do you compost?"

He kept walking; pretending not to hear.

Jarvis felt there was something weird about Le Trou Du Cul. The people here struck him as bizarre. But he needed to be here. He was 'hiding in plain sight' as they say. Running away from his old life. So far, all the people he'd met seemed odd. Right after moving in he could feel something bizarre about the place. The woods on the south side of Le Trou Du Cul was creepy rather than scenic. The people (those he'd met and those he'd simply passed by here and there) appeared *off* somehow. And the man-made lake, with the fog constantly raising from it, seemed eerie rather than relaxing, like something from an old Hammer horror movie.

The large man in 4-B—Louis (the food scientist, apparently)—played Christmas music, despite it being July. He'd heard the elderly man, on the floor below him, complaining to the super (Sanchez, or was it Santiago?) that his apartment had gotten smaller over the year he'd been here. And the woman on the second floor, Lula, had been drunk the few times he'd seen her around.

Yes, all of these things added up to nothing on the surface. But he couldn't help but feel something strange was afoot. Was just being paranoid? After all, this was just any other apartment complex. He'd soon realize how wrong he was.

TWO

Summer - Earth Goddess, Master, Spiritual Superior

Summer went back to her apartment. The new guy was an asshole. How dare he tell *her* about health! She lit some sage that she'd bought at a Meditation Moe's store, to clear the negative energy Jarvis left on her aura. The sage had been very expensive, but the cashier had assured her it came from a Persian rain forest, gathered by the natives there in a 'spiritual fashion' and was also a fair-trade product. She put on some authentic African chant music, by the popular Harvard University Choir (made-up of all upper-class white kids) and recorded in one of the most expensive recording studios in the world, and sat down to meditate. She asked that her spirt guide come to her and lead her in life's journey. She'd done this for months with no luck contacting anything but numb legs.

Just as she was about to give up, there was a crash from the living room. The photo of Maharigege Sanhaditteha—a great and wise yogi whom she'd never heard of and had no idea what he did—had fallen, leaving a large hole in the wall.

As she went to clean up the glass, a voice   came from the hole.

"Mindy Weinstein?" It called. Her real name.

She stood, stunned. "What?"

"I'm sorry…Summer?"

"Hello?" She asked, looking into the hole. A vestigial dumbwaiter. The chain tightened. Moved. And that is when the celestial being known as Slymind Braintwist appeared. Summer fell to her knees. She'd always known she was special, a spiritual master. And now she was being summoned for her higher calling. Finally! She went into a coughing fit.

"That's some cough you got on you, kid," the angel said. He came through the hole. He was little, pink, and fuzzy. He was beautiful.

"I just need to drink more dandelion tea," Summer said, getting up from her knees. The angel smiled a wide grin of rainbow teeth.

"That tea is piss. But you drink that too!" he said, laughing.

He was free at last. The woman had broken the wall a bit when putting in the nail for her photo of some brown berry-eater who lived in a cave and blamed capitalism for the fact that he ate a bowl of dirt for dinner every evening. He was free to roam the earth, or at least Le Trou Du Cul, once again! He'd lived in Heck for long enough. He was a demon free to raise heck on earth! True, raising heck was not the same as raising hell but it would have to do. People thought that all demons were from Hell, not true. There was a domain before Hell…Heck. And while Slymind Braintwist could not possess people, make people kill one another or coerce people to turn from God, he *could* annoy the living shit out of them!

The being rubbed his pink furry hands together. Sparkles flew. He produced a vile that also sparkled.

"Drink this and not your piss. It's an elixir straight from Heck," he said in a high voice.

"Oh God! Thank you, thank you."

"I have to go now. Drink that every evening before bed. You will feel worse before you feel better."

"Thank you!"

***

Louis Greene was listening to the Barry Manilow Christmas record on his phone. The irony of a Jew recording a Christmas record was not completely lost on him, but it was a great record. He waddled through the woods. Bobbi had not joined him here in some time. She was a good wife but was not interested in searching for mythological creatures. At first, she'd humored him, accompanying him and looking at it more as a walk than a search. God knew Louis needed the exercise. Bobbi was still an attractive woman and he'd really, really let himself go. She was happy he was walking around. But over the weeks she saw his hobby grow into an obsession. And while the glimpse he'd caught of the creature a month ago was just that, a glimpse, he knew what he had seen. It was sasquatch.

He moved a little deeper into the woods. The air became thick with a mulch smell. Damper. Then…a sound. A twig breaking. He pulled the earbuds from his ears. Manillow's version of *It's Cold Outside* died. He put his phone into camera mode. But all he saw through the screen was mostly blackness. He took a few steps forward. And there was no question, this was a sasquatch. Its back was to him. A hairy creature, yet he could see skin through the hair.

"Hello…." Louis attempted to make contact. The creature turned around. Though its body was full of dark hair, it had an almost humanoid face. Then he realized this was some sort of crossbreed sasquatch/human. Another one appeared. They were both…crossed of Bigfoot and the ubiquitous porn star, Ron Jeremy! A little, orange creature jumped from one Ron Jeremy to the other. It was the size of a small monkey and jumped to the ground, squatting. It made a huge pile of dung. The little thing was indeed similar to a monkey, but not any monkey from this world. Louis fumbled with the camera on his phone—attempting to brighten the picture—and while he was not looking, the little thing threw one of its turds at him. The shit smashed across Louis's face and he dropped the phone. The little thing laughed and actually spoke.

"Up your ass, fat boy!"

Louis snapped off a lone photo just as Bigfoot/Ron Jeremy creatures as they were running away. Of course, the photo was of one of the creatures from behind. And blurry.

Jarvis was looking around the mailbox area. If anyone had found him, he saw no sign of it. This place was just out of the way enough. He heard a commotion heading his way. He pulled his cap down, but it was only Louis and Bobbi Greene.

"It's nothing, Louis. Who would believe anything from that," Bobbi was saying.

"I know. But I *saw* it. It *spoke* to me! Well, the baby did."

"There's a baby, now? The Ron Jeremy creatures have a baby?" Bobbi asked.

"Hey, guys," Jarvis smiled politely.

"Hey. Look at this!" Louis held out his phone. It was a blurry photo. Of what, Jarvis did not know.

"What is it?"

"Bigfoot, of course. Well, a Ron Jeremy\Bigfoot…I think. Here's the left arm." Louis pointed to something indistinguishable in the photo.

"Louis, leave him alone." Bobbi said, hugging her husband with a kiss.

"I'll get proof," Louis said.

"I know you will, lover."

"I love you," Louis said to his wife.

"I love you, too, hunk."

Louis riffled through his fanny pack and pulled out a small bag and handed it to Jarvis.

"Here, have some candy."

"Thanks," Jarvis grimaced, looking at the white chocolate and ketchup truffles.

He made his way back to his apartment and there was a man—dressed in a cheap suit and a ratty, yellow fedora—standing by his door. Jarvis began to turn around, but the man had already seen him.

"Kyle Jarvis?" the man asked.

"Yea."

The man opened his wallet and produced a badge.

"Detective Nick Black."

"Yes?"

"I'd like to ask you a few questions."

"About?"

"Oh, about this apartment complex."

"I'm actually new here. Is there a reason you want to speak with me? Maybe you want to question someone who's lived here longer."

"I will be. But I would also like the perspective of someone like yourself, who's new."

"How can I help?"

Detective Black fished a pack of smokes from his jacket. Jarvis noticed that the pack was plain and white with only the word 'CIGARETTES" in bold black letters. Odd.

"Well I have been told that there are strange things going on here."

"Strange, how?"

"You tell me."

"Sorry, I have not noticed anything strange. But as I said, I am new here."

"Why did you move here?"

"Sorry? I don't know how to answer that."

"Why did you choose Le Trou Du Cul of all the places you could have moved?"

"The price was reasonable, and I liked it."

"What do you do for a living?"

"I work in a mail room for a payroll company. Why?"

"A mail room. And you can handle the rent?"

"I saved."

"Have you seen Bigfoot here on the complex grounds?"

"'Bigfoot'? Is that what this is about?"

"Maybe."

"No, I have not. Am I under some sort of suspicion, Detective Black?"

"Relax. As I said, I will be questioning a number of people here, as well."

"Have we met?" Jarvis asked. The detective looked familiar. His voice sounded familiar as well.

"I don't think so. Have you ever been in trouble with the law?"

"If you don't mind I am kind of busy," Jarvis avoided and put his key in the door.

"Are you planning on leaving town?"

What was this? This detective Black was like a cop out of a bad movie, completely stereotypical. It almost felt like a put on, some kind of joke.

"No, I'm not leaving town."

"Good. One thing I will give you, Jarvis. You sure come up with answers. And quick."

"Well it's easy when you tell the truth."

"Yea, you keep telling yourself that. See you around," Black parted.

Jarvis watched the man leave. He looked towards the woods. They appeared deeper than they had been the day before, denser too. How was that possible?

THREE

And Thy Shite Shall Be Stirred

The little demon pulled the chain and attempted to get into all the apartments, but it would not work. He could only enter the homes that the dumbwaiter ran through and that was only four apartments. But he could still influence those in apartments that he did not have access to. Sure, he could not *directly* communicate with them, but he could irritate them just the same. He was going to put Le Trou Du Cul in chaos as he had all those years ago. There are portals to Hell, as any number of horror movies and novels were testament to. And there was a portal to Heck, as well—known as the *Asshole of the Universe*. He took a deep breath and rubbed his little pink feet together. Tiny stars flew from the pink fuzz.

"*Small and hard, red like shard,*" he said and giggled.

***

Louis Greene and his wife, Bobbi had lived in Le Trou Du Cul for over twenty years. A food additive chemist and homemaker who had simple tastes, simples lives and still enjoyed one another's company. Louis did little for recreation other than his never-ending search for the supernatural, (aliens, ghosts, sea creatures and, of course, Sasquatch) as well as eating. At 372 pounds you could bet he ate a lot. People thought he was strange because he liked to listen to Christmas music year-round. He saw nothing odd about this whatsoever. And Bobbi loved him despite his weight and idiosyncrasies. They were sickeningly in love.

He put on coffee and was on his way to take his morning piss when a pain like nothing he'd ever felt, shot up from his left foot and throughout his entire body—even reaching his very soul. He fell.

"Christ almighty in heaven! Fuck me sideways!"

He rolled around on the living room floor. Bobbi ran out of the bedroom to find him there.

"Oh my god, a heart attack!" Bobbi said, looking down on him.

"No! My foot!"

"I knew your heart would eventually give out!"

"No! My Goddamn fucking foot!"

"Your heart—*foot*?" Bobbi asked.

Louis grabbed a chubby foot and brought it as close to his face as he could, to see the damage.

"—the fuck?"

"What happened?"

The pain was beginning to subside. There, stuck to his foot, was a red LEGO. How the hell had this gotten in their apartment? They had no kids and never had any visitors. How was this possible? Bobbi must have brought it in. She was always doing arts and crafts bullshit. Scrapbooking, making knick-knacks and leaving shit all over the apartment.

"What is that?"

"Why the fuck would you bring this shit in here?"

"Are you cursing at *me*?"

"Goddamn right. What bullshit nonsense were you making with fucking LEGO?"

"LEGO?"

"Yea. I stepped on a cock-sucking, mother-fucking LEGO. Christ, the pain! What were you doing fucking around with LEGO?"

Louis never cursed. Bobbi was shocked.

"Do you hear yourself?"

"Loud and clear!"

"What the fuck would I be doing with LEGO, you fat fuck?!"

Bobbi had never spoken to him like this. What nerve! And after putting this thing on the floor for him to trip on. Maybe she was trying to hurt him. Maybe she even wanted it to *kill* him.

"You want me dead, is that it?"

"What?"

"Oh, I'm on to you..."

He got up and threw the infernal thing into the garbage. His mood was shot.

***

As promised, Jarvis found the flyer for Marlene's one-woman-show in his mailbox this morning. It promised an elegant night of theater as had not been witnessed in years. There was also another flyer containing the blurry photo of the hairy thing Louis had taken, and stated that caution needed to be taken as sasquatch—he had left out the Ron Jeremy part—was now confirmed to be roaming in the area surrounding Le Trou Du Cul.

Summer arrived at the mailbox and made an "uhh" sound, as if seeing him was akin to seeing something foul a dog might have dragged in. She was in her pajamas. God help him, she looked adorable. But he disliked the woman immensely, no matter how cute she could appear. Jarvis gave a sarcastic, too wide grin. The woman looked tired and refused to make eye contact.

"Good morning," he said.

"You know, you really—" she started but then began coughing.

"Are you okay—"

"I'm fine! Better than fine."

"You sound—"

"Never you mind."

"Okay. I'd hate to see you get pneumonia," He muttered, thinking it would totally serve her right.

"My celestial guide is taking me through this."

"You still may want to see a doctor—"

"Go to Heck!"

"Huh?"

"No, go to Hell!"

A man walked by with a tray holding four cups of coffee. He stopped and gave a wet, awful sounding sneeze.

"Jesus Christ! Cover your mouth when you sneeze," Summer screamed. She produced a vile from her pocked and drank the thick sparkly liquid from within.

"I'm holding this," the man said, indicating the tray.

"You fuckin' savage!" Summer turned to run away, screaming again.

***

"Summon confusion with all my might, with drink and sex the two shall fight."

Lula Sykes was sleeping off a fuck of a hangover when her cell phone dinged. And dinged. And dinged. She finally got up, rubbing her eyes to see the screen. Kurt, the guy who lived on the second floor—with his roommate, Brian, whom she had slept with a few weeks ago (a mistake)—was texting her over and over. The texts got worse and worse.

HEY
ARE U UP ?
I AM THINKING ABOUT YOU
ANSWER ME
YOU THERE
HELLO. HELLO! HELLO!!!!
I HAVE TO TELL U SOMETHIN
ANSWER ME PLEASE
OKAY
I THINK I LOVE YOU
NO I DO LOVE YOU
HELLO??
NOTHING?
ARE U KIDDING??
ANSWER ME YOU DUMB BITCH!

What fucking nerve! Lula got up and put on jeans and a shirt. heading downstairs to the little prick's apartment, fists clenched. She pounded on the door. Pounded again. The door opened. Kurt!

"Hey..."

"*Hey* your ass, fucker! Are you nuts?"

"What? Lula, what the hell?"

"You text me one more time and I will kick you in your tiny balls!"

"I didn't text you," Kurt said. Was she drunk?

"You tiny prick loser. It was a one-night-thing. Understand?"

"You're Goddamn right it was a one-night-thing. You think I'd fuck you twice, you chubby lush?!"

"You cocksucker!"

"Get the fuck out of here, you crazy bitch!"

And as promised, Lula kicked Kurt in the nuts. Thank God her aim was a bit off and she caught a little of his thigh first, dulling the shot. But her foot connected enough.

"Fuck me!" Kurt wailed.

"Don't ever call or text me again, little dick!"

"You fucking drunk!"

After recovering, Kurt got in his car and took off. He was going to leave the apartment for the day. If Lula came back to bother him, Brian could deal with her.

***

"Drive him nuts with all I got, earth and water cold and hot."

In apartment 2-D, Edward Holman was attempting to take a shower but the water kept getting colder and colder. He twisted the knob all the way to the right but still no hot. The water kept turning off and back on. With a head full of shampoo, the water went out completely.

"What the fuck!"

Then it came on full blast and piping hot, scalding his ass. He jumped from the shower, taking the curtain and pole down with him and banging his head on the wall.

He did the best he could toweling drying his hair. He grabbed his phone, realizing that he had no number for a damn super. He began looking for the welcome package he'd received from Le Trou Du Cul when they'd first moved in. He could hear a woman screaming at a man in the hallway but was not concerned. He was opening and banging drawers and throwing things all around when his wife, Jena came in.

"What the hell is going on out here?" Jena said.

"What does it look like?"

"I have no idea! You're dripping all over the floor."

"I'm looking for our welcome packet."

"What welcome packet?"

"The packet welcoming us to Mars!"

"What the hell are you babbling about? Why are you all soapy?"

"Why do you think?"

"I have no idea," she said again.

"The goddamn water is all fucked up."

"I just took a shower before and it was fine."

"Well bully for you. It ain't fine now!"

"Stop yelling at me!"

"I'm yelling but I am not yelling *at* you."

"Yes, you are."

"Do you have the number for Sanchez?"

"Who the hell is Sanchez?"

"The super."

"You mean Suarez? Or is it Santos?"

"What?"

"I thought it was Sanchez. Or is it Santiago?" Jena said.

"Sanchez, Santos, Suarez, Santiago! Just call the little spic and have the goddamn wet-back fix the water!"

"Ed!" In all their years together, she had never heard her husband use a racial slur.

"What? Do you have the number for the little brown beaner or not?"

And they began to bicker and fight about who was supposed to know the number of the landlord or the super. She accused Ed of being a closet racist. And from there she gave her husband some shit about his temper. And he let her know that his temper had always been fine before he had married her, the overbearing bitch. Then, she somehow brought his mother into it. And the little pink devil jumped for joy.

***

"Lose your mind the man shall think and laugh and grin as his world does shrink."

Craig Floyd had first thought he was losing his mind. Or that it may have been the new meds he was on. But now there was no denying it. His apartment was getting smaller. Not figuratively, as in he was gathering more stuff and therefore the apartment *seemed* smaller. But the place was physically shrinking. He'd measured his bedroom before going to bed last night and this morning it was almost a full square foot smaller. At almost eighty-two-years-old he also thought he was getting senile. But last night his bathroom had had a bath and today it was only a shower stall. He'd considered calling his daughter, but she was a four-hour flight away with a husband and two daughters of her own. She had her own problems. He would have called the super, Santiago. Or was it Suarez? He could not remember. But the faggy Hispanic had not been around in weeks. Probably out galivanting with his boyfriend, Craig thought.

"What is happening?" Craig asked himself.

***

Louis Green sat by the man-made lake. He was typing on his laptop, writing a report of his Bigfoot evidence. He also had his phone's camera ready, the lock screen disabled. Better to be away from the apartment today. His wife was still pissed at him and his damn foot still hurt from that infernal LEGO.

He looked to the woods. It was getting deeper. New trees where here too, he was sure. But how? Then he realized he was wrong. The woods were not only getting deeper, but they were also getting *closer*. Closing in on the complex.

A few yards away a man was walking a dog. A smartly dressed young woman passed by with a clipboard and asked if he was interested in switching to a faster, more reliable, cheaper ISP. He wasn't.

"Hey, Louis! Just the guy I was looking for. And here he is, clear as day and twice as ugly." It was Buddy Horn. He was with that bratty son of his. The boy was finishing an ice cream sandwich, his mouth and hands a sticky mess.

"Hey, Buddy. Timmy," Louis said.

"Hey, guess what? I saw Bigfoot yesterday. I thought I should let you know," Buddy said.

"What? You did! Did you get a photo?!"

"Of course, he did. Didn't you, dad?" Timmy said with a smirk.

"Oh yea."

"That's great! Lemme see!"

"Yea. The whole Big Foot family came over for dinner last night. Liz made a pot roast!" Buddy said, and he and his son cracked up, walking away.

"Assholes," Louis said to himself.

Buddy stopped walking.

"What's that?"

"Nothing," Louis said.

"You're damn right 'nothing', fatso," Buddy said. Timmy threw his ice cream wrapper at the man as they walked away.

Louis fumed.

"Hey!" Someone was yelling at the man with the dog.

"Yea?" The dog man said.

"Pick up that shit," the man said, pointing to a huge pile of orange shit.

It's the little-Bigfoot's shit, Louis thought.

"That's not my dog's shit. You pick it up."

"I just watched him do it."

"My little dog can't make a shit like that. It's bigger than he is."

"I just watched him do it."

"You saw that turd tumble out of *this* dog's ass?" The man said, pointing to his dog. The dog looked embarrassed, as if he understood the crazy conversation.

"I sure as hell did."

"Bullshit. Prove it's his"

"Where else did that turd come from?"

"I don't know. Maybe your mother came out here and squatted down and shit while she was blowing a group of niggers!" the dog-walker shouted. The dog began barking at his master's raised voice.

"Yea? I got your mother in my apartment right now. Me and my buddies are gangbanging her...in the ass!" And just as the men were about to come face-to-face, the woman with the clipboard came running between them, screaming. Another woman, someone from the complex whose name Louis did not know, was chasing her.

"I'll push that clipboard up your ass, bitch!"

The woman who worked for the superior ISP was gone. The woman chasing her, too, walked away.

Thank God that was over, Louis thought. Someone near him lit up a cigar and the wind blew the smoke right into his face. He ignored it, hoping the wind would eventually change direction. Of course, it didn't. After ten minutes, Louis approached the man.

Say what you mean, but don't say it meanly, Louis thought. Something his therapist had taught him.

"Excuse me, Sir?"

The cigar guy looked at him with suspicion.

"Yea."

"Sorry but the smoke is blowing right at me."

The guy took the cigar from his mouth and spit a fleck of loose tobacco from his tongue.

"I don't tell the wind where to blow."

Louis picked up his laptop, beach chair and phone, heading to the other side of the lake. A skinny woman with a hard face was texting on her phone. Louis got back to writing his paper. Just as he was getting into a groove there was a loud sound—some stupid dance song that was being played everywhere and by everyone that week. The skinny, mad-looking woman answered her phone.

"Marybeth Weitz-Hanson," she said, loudly.

"No. No! I told him not to expense those reports! Because *I* said so, that's why! Bullshit! No—"

He kept losing his concentration and typing the same sentence over and over.

"Ma'am, can you keep it down, please?"

"What?"

"You're a little loud—"

"Shouldn't you be looking for Bigfoot, fat boy?" She said before dismissing him and turning back to her phone call: "I don't know. Some fuckin' loser...."

Louis Green closed up his laptop. He folded his beach chair and put his phone in his pocket, then walked over to the woman. In one quick motion he grabbed her phone and tossed it into the lake.

Stunned, the woman stood for a moment and ran. And then Louis saw it as clear as day. The head of a sea creature rose from the lake. It's small head and tapered neck hinted at something much larger and prehistoric beneath the water's surface. He fumbled for his phone, but the thing was gone, leaving only a ripple in the water as proof of its appearance.

"Son-of-a-bitch!" Louis roared.

FOUR

Marlene Davis - First Woman of The Theatre

She was dosing off watching a soap opera—a storyline about a man sleeping with his fifth wife's daughter, who was also sleeping with his son, who was also sleeping with his father's wife—when the plaster fell. She stirred and went to the wall. Furry pink hands were breaking through the sheetrock.

"Marlene Davis, the great actress. It's an honor to meet such a renowned artist," Sly said and bowed his little body. Marlene looked at the creature.

"What are you?"

"A demon."

He did not look evil at all.

"Demon?"

"I can give you the adulation of the audience again."

"What?"

"You want to go back to your theatre days?"

"Yes, the stage."

"I can assist."

"What…oh, of course," Marlene said. A demon could give her beauty and youth again, right?

"I cannot make you young again," the creature said, reading her mind. "But I can try and conjure something from your glory days."

"Yes!"

"What can I do?"

"I have my big comeback show tonight. Maybe you can help me succeed!"

"Oh, Ms. Davis. Certainly, a seasoned professional such as yourself does not need help from Slymind Braintwist, with theatre, of all things."

"But it's been so long since I have owned the stage."

"Of course. Here are my words for you. The cute pink demon closed his eyes and chanted.

"Take the stage and show the prude, the power of beauty of a woman nude."

Marlene promptly passed out.

***

"With eyes blind and all they say, let the chips fall where they may."

"Where are the chips?" Chuck Wolfe shouted from the kitchen.

"What?" Verna asked.

"The chips. Where are they?"

"What chips?"

"Those Thanksgiving chips that Louis gave us. You know, one chip tastes like turkey, another is potatoes...I like the gravy ones."

"Check the pantry."

"I am. They aren't here. Did you eat them?"

"No. I wouldn't eat that shit."

"Well where did they go?"

"In the pantry."

"I'm looking in the blanin' pantry and there are not here."

"Yes, they are."

Chuck removed everything from the pantry shelves and the chips were *not* here!

He put everything back. He repeated the process to be sure.

"I can't find therm. Verna, show me the damn chips, would ya?"

She stopped folding laundry. Her husband could not do anything himself anymore and she'd had about enough of it. She came into the kitchen and found Chuck standing at the pantry looking angry and confused. She walked past him, and the chips were right in front of his stupid face. She pulled the bag out and handed it to him.

"Get your eyes checked."

"What the…" Chuck felt like a fool.

He grabbed the chips and poured himself an iced tea. He turned on the TV to the local news station. While it was supposed to be nothing but local news, it was getting a little *too* local lately. The news these days hardly covered anything outside of their little town. He could not remember the name of the town. Was he going nuts?

He settled into his chair and struggled to open the bag of chips. The bag seemed impenetrable.

"Oh, for cryin' out loud."

He applied more pressure and the bag opened, split down the middle. His left hand flew and knocked his glass of tea off the end table, chips flew all over the living room. There were at least four times the amount of chips that could possibly have been in the bag, all over the floor.

"Mother fucker! I have nothing in this miserable life. I can't even have a few chips and iced tea!"

He got down on his hands and knees, cleaning up the mess.

"What?" Verna said. He could hear her heading toward the living room.

"Nothing! Don't come in here!"

She appeared.

"What the hell did you do?"

"I dumped my fucking iced tea on the floor and now I'm rolling around in chips for the fuck of it!"

"Well clean it up."

On the TV was the outside of Le Trou Du Cul. The news was getting more local still. It seemed the news was only of Le Trou Du Cul the last few days. But Chuck was too pissed to notice.

***

Buddy had caught him in the laundry room that afternoon and sandbagged him with the loaded question 'what are you doing after dinner tonight?' Jarvis had no lie at the ready. And as a result, he was now heading out to the courtyard to play corn hole with the crowd. Unlike the jocular group he had watched from his window yesterday, everyone appeared to be in a pissy mood.

Louis and Bobbi Greene were here. Chuck and Verna were here as well. Summer even joined them but was sure to keep her distance from him. Jarvis could hear Louis saying something about "Bigfoot" to a younger man. Bobbi rolled her eyes. They appeared less like the *in love* couple he'd met, and Bobbi seemed sick of her husband's obsession.

Buddy, Liz and Timmy joined everyone. Buddy ran right over to Chuck, who was setting up the corn hole board, the two alpha males running the show.

"You're doing it all wrong, numb-nuts," Buddy said.

"Oh, well thank God you're here to teach me how to do it right."

Jarvis had to laugh. Anything anyone did, Buddy Horn was happy to tell you how he did it before you. Faster than you. Cheaper than you. Better than you.

Buddy leaned over to Louis, who was sipping a beer.

"Hey Louis. You love Christmas songs, right?" Buddy asked.

"I sure do—"

"Here's one for ya," Buddy said, cupping his balls. "'I have *balls* that jingle jangle jingle'," He sang and hooted.

"My *balls* jingle. Jingle BALLS!" Timmy said.

"Very funny," Louis replied.

"Here's another: 'Chestnuts roasting on an open fire, my nuts resting on your chin'," Buddy sang in a slow, low baritone.

As Louis joined her husband and Buddy with the setting up of the corn hole, Verna sidled up to Jarvis.

"Hey, Jarvis."

"Hi, Verna."

"I didn't know you played corn hole," She said, coming close. She smelled good, like the ocean and something taboo.

"I don't play. But Buddy asked me to join." Verna held her phone up.

"I collect salt and pepper shakers. Here, look," she said in a lowered voice.

She swiped past an insanely large collection of the things. Each photo had a caption. There was a photo of basic diner shakers named 'the American Classic,' figurines shakers, Smurf shakers, shakers from all countries and regions, and all shapes and sizes. Finally, she swiped to a photo of a pair of cock salt & pepper shakers. Verna stopped on it.

"Oh…." Jarvis said, embarrassed.

"I got these at an adult shop three years ago," Verna said with a smirk.

"I didn't know they even made…."

"Cocks?" Verna asked.

"Yea."

"These are Chuck's favorite. They are *my* favorite, too."

"Oh…."

"These are big. The biggest shakers I own. Do *you* look like that?" She purred in his ear. Jarvis felt heat in his groin.

"I…."

"Chuck is small. He's gotten disinterested in me, as well," Verna said.

"Ready!" Buddy yelled.

"Hey, corn hole time," Jarvis said, relieved.

Liz looked at her own phone.

"Oh no."

"What?" Buddy asked.

"Lula is working late—she's not going to make it."

"Oh, what a tragedy," Buddy said.

"What do you have against her?" Liz asked.

"Oh, I don't know, she's drinking all the time," Buddy said.

"Oh, and you're not?" Liz asked.

"Honey, I'm a man. It's different."

"Oh please," Summer said. Buddy ignored her.

"And seriously, what kind of a woman has a threesome with two men?"

"I should never have told you that. And, for your information, she didn't sleep with two men; it was a guy and his girlfriend," Liz said.

"How's that?" Buddy asked.

"Lula didn't have sex with two *men*; it was a man and a girl."

"Oh…really? You're kidding?" Buddy said, smiling.

"Oh, now it's okay?"

"I guess…."

"You're a pig. "

"Did you hear she got robbed again?" Bobbi interrupted.

"No. The store?" Liz asked.

"Yea. She's really scared," Bobbi said.

"What kind of an idiot robs a fabric store? Jesus, I mean every piece of cloth in that place costs sixty cents a mile. What did he get away with, eleven dollars?" Buddy laughed.

"Christ, Buddy, that's not the point." Liz rolled her eyes. "Such an idiot."

They began playing. Summer even joined in. Everyone drank beer and laughed. But as the game went on, the vibe became less friendly. Buddy, Louis and Chuck began to bicker about the rules.

"You're tossing the sack all wrong," Louis said.

"Toss this sack." Buddy cupped his balls again. It seemed his favorite move.

"You got nothing there, Buddy," Louis laughed.

"Yea, Louis? That's not what your mother says. Speaking of your mother, can you tell her to stick to one shade of lipstick, my Mr. Happy is starting to look like a fuckin' rainbow," Buddy laughed, and threw a bean bag. "Point!"

"Yea right. You still don't understand the game," Louis said.

"Hey, did a cop question any of you guys?" Jarvis asked.

"Cop?" Buddy asked.

"Yea. Detective Black. He was here earlier and was asking me stuff about the complex."

"What kind of stuff," Chuck wanted to know.

"Nothing really. If I had seen anything strange around here."

"Strange how," Bobbi questioned.

"He really didn't say. He asked if I'd seen Bigfoot."

"Bigfoot! What did he want to know? Are the cops getting in on this? Big Foot is mine!" Louis began to get heated.

Chuck ignored the conversation. "Did I ever tell you guys about when my platoon plane crashed? About my old Army buddy, Lefty?"

"Everyone's heard this, Chuck," Verna said.

"No, Jarvis never heard it."

"You survived a plane crash?" Jarvis asked.

"Oh boy," Verna said.

"Damn right I did. We were in a plane, three of us. We're in the plane, a small shitty thing. We were off course and had nowhere to land, in the middle of nowhere. We were tired.

Finally, we ran out of gas. We tried to land and crashed. Me and Benny were okay…but Lefty didn't fare so well…"

"The other guy died?" Jarvis asked.

"Well…after thirty hours or so Benny decides we should eat the dead guy. But you know me, Verna, I'm not ready to eat, I could never eat before six. So, Benny gets an ax from what's left of the plane."

"Oh God," Summer grimaced.

"He rips through young Marty—Lefty's leg. He cooks the damn thing on an open fire. He is eating. I'm watching him. And all of a sudden, we hear a moan…sounds like it's coming from the plane. Benny puts the leg down. We both think it's a ghost; a ghoulish moan. Would you believe it's Lefty?"

"His ghost?" Summer's eyes are saucers.

"The man whose leg was just cut off?" Jarvis asked.

"Yep…he was unconscious—not dead! Benny took the damn kid's leg off while he was knocked-out! He became 'Lefty' after that!" Chuck laughed.

"Ha! I love that story," Buddy roared.

"He ate the leg," Timmy laughed.

"God, that's sick," Summer said, wrinkling up her nose.

"Well you're a vegan so what do you know?" Buddy teased her.

They continued drinking beer and playing. At one-point Chuck got in Louis's face over a toss but mellowed when Louis offered him some horse radish flavored cookies. The bickering went on. Summer looked at Jarvis a few times and he gave her a wave of the hand to leave it alone. It was turning to dusk.

"So back when I was playing varsity football, we had this little fellow who brought us water and took care of our equipment, that kind of shit. He was a real fairy. He was out in the open and shit. No closet for this queer. No shame. Floating around the school gay as a day in May," Buddy said.

"Yea, a little fairy-boy?" Chuck asked.

"Oh yea. He'd prance around in little short-shorts and everything."

"Yea? Little tight shorts? What did he look like?" Chuck asked.

"Like a little queer, that's what he looked like," Buddy said, annoyed to be distracted.

"Suck bigots," Summer took a sip of her drink.

"This story again?" Liz asked, returning from getting a fresh beer.

"They never heard it."

"Yea, I never heard it. So, tell us about this little twink," Chuck said.

"Huh? *Twink*?"

"Uh, the little fairy-boy, I mean," Chuck said.

"Well, he was great with all our equipment, washed the jocks and everything. Probably sniffed 'em before washing 'em," Buddy laughed.

"Oh yea. You sure as shit know he was sniffing them jocks," Chuck said.

"Anyway, every Friday around four, this fruitcake goes into the bathroom at the gym. A lot of people are gone. He'd be all packed up for the day—has his coat on and duffle bag over his shoulder like a girl with a purse. And he's in there a while. Every damn Friday. So, we get the idea to see what he's doing. But anytime I go in there all I see is his shoes and his bag on the floor of the stall."

"I bet he's doing some gay shit in there. Please tell me he was pulling some gay shit in there, Buddy," Chuck said, a little too excitedly.

"Oh, yea. So, after weeks of this I finally had enough. I bring a screwdriver in with me. Sure enough: first stall. Shoes and bag on the floor. So quietly as could be, I slip the latch of the stall—"

"Yea, yea..." Chuck was on the edge of his seat.

"—and not only is this fag in the stall, but one of our players is in there with him. One of *our* fucking players. He's in the stall with the fairy. They are facing each other, pants down, hard-ons out, a real swordfight, jerking each other off!" Buddy said.

"I knew it! I just fucking knew it!" Chuck said.

"Wait," Bobbi said, "I thought you said there was only the one guy in there when you looked under the stall?"

"Well our fullback would go in there earlier and wait. Then the fruit would get in the stall with him and our player would step *into* the duffel bag on the floor. So, anyone going in only sees one pair of shoes!"

"A bag, huh? That's genius!" Chuck declares.

"God, you love telling that story," Liz said.

"Why wouldn't I?" Buddy asked.

"Yea, why not? It's a *great* story!" Chuck said.

"Yea, real funny," Summer agreed.

"Them fags were playing with each other's ding-a-lings," Timmy cackled.

They played some more. Jarvis watched as the competitive nature of the men came out. They drank more beer and the squabbling grew.

"You toss like a girl," Chuck said to Bobbi and laughed.

"What is that supposed to mean?" Summer wanted to know.

"It means women can't play sports as good as a man," Chuck replied.

"What bullshit."

"C'mon, Jarvis. Back up the men here," Chuck said.

"Yea, Jarvis," Summer said.

"Well...."

"Don't even," Summer put a hand on her slim hip.

"Yea, Jarvis. Are men better at sports than women or not?" Buddy asked, enjoying himself.

"I'm not saying a thing."

"Smart move," Summer glared.

Louis tossed the bean bag.

"Hey, that was not a point, Buddy," Louis said.

"Your ass."

Buddy was explaining to Chuck about the deer he'd shot while hunting last weekend.

"I was out last Sunday, looking for some action," Buddy said.

"What kind of action?" Chuck asked.

"Let's just say I bagged this big black buck," Buddy boosted.

"Really?" Chuck asked nervously.

"Oh yea. Beautiful big black buck."

"Shh...keep your voice down. Where did you meet him?" Chuck asked.

"*Meet him*? I *hunted* for him."

"Where can I hunt for a nice big black buck around here?" Chuck whispered.

"The woods."

"Oh yea, I've heard of that...Does Liz know?"

"Sure, I showed her the pictures."

"Really? She's cool with that?"

"Chuck, what the hell are you talking about? I've invited you hunting a million times and you're never interested. Said you don't like venison."

Chuck shook himself.

"Oh yea...deer...buck...never mind."

"I shot the fucker right in the noggin'. Dropped him in one."

"That's disgusting," Summer said.

"Please."

"You feel like a big man killing a defenseless animal?"

"Look here, sister. They don't have enough food supply. They are going to die anyway. They won't survive the winter."

Summer looked at Jarvis. What was he today—the voice of reason? But Summer looked so damn cute.

"Such nonsense. Of course, they'll survive the winter," she said.

"No, they won't," Buddy shouted.

"Jarvis, have you ever heard that?" Summer asked.

"Well they definitely have a better chance of surviving if you're not shooting at them," Jarvis chimed in. He'd meant it as a joke, but Summer looked impressed.

"That's right, Jarvis," Summer said and touched his arm. His cock jumped in his jeans. He did not like the woman. But he had to admit she looked like she'd be good in bed. Not that he was here to get laid. And Summer hated him, he knew. He had to keep his mind clear.

"C'mon, Jarvis. Don't go pussy on me," Buddy said.

"I'm just not sure your theory holds up, Buddy," Jarvis said. Summer smiled.

"And 'pussy' is a misogynist term," Summer said.

"That's true," Jarvis agreed.

"Oh, shit. I get it now. You're trying to get in the hippie's pants," Buddy said. He held up his hands. "Say no more."

"Oh God," Summer said.

Verna glared at Summer. She was a dirty hippie, but she was young, pretty, and thin.

"Buddy, can you just play and stop being a dick?" Liz asked.

Buddy laughed and threw a beanbag. "Another two points!"

"What? You missed," Louis said.

"What are you blind, chubs?" Buddy asked.

"You missed. And you're not exactly thin yourself," Louis said, sadly.

"You weren't even looking. You're too busy watching the woods for fuckin' Bigfoot!" Buddy laughed.

"He's in there," Louis said.

"Enough with this Bigfoot shit," Bobbi said.

"I thought you supported me?" Louis said, hurt.

"I do, honey. But this is getting crazy," Bobbi said.

"Why don't you two just hook up?" Buddy remarked to Summer and Jarvis.

"Buddy, stop," Jarvis said.

"Yea, Buddy. Mind your own damn business," Verna smiled at Jarvis.

"Why do you keep looking at him," Chuck asked his wife.

"Looking at who?" Verna asked.

"At Jarvis! You also want to fuck him!"

"Oh shit," Buddy roared.

"What do you mean *also*?" Summer demanded.

"You did miss that shot. Louis is right," Chuck added.

"What? Are you blind, too?" Buddy joked.

"He got it in," Timmy said.

"Mind your own business, punk!" Louis said.

"Hey! Here, tell me if I get this one in the hole," Buddy yelled and wailed a bean bag at Chuck's ass.

"Son-of-a-bitch," Chuck said and picked up a bean bag, throwing it at Buddy, who ducked, and the bean bag hit Verna square in the face.

"You prick," Verna wailed and ran for Buddy. Liz was on her in a flash.

Louis and Bobbi went about breaking Liz and Verna up and Jarvis jumped in to stop Chuck and Buddy. Jarvis was hit in the eye but still managed to stop the men from killing each other. He then jumped in to stop the cat fight. Verna grabbed Jarvis' hands and placed it on one of her large breasts. She managed to make it look accidental.

"Get your fuckin' hands of my wife's tits!" Chuck roared.

Summer screamed.

"Let the girls go at it, Jarvis. C'mon ladies. Rip each other's clothes off!" Buddy shouted. "Summer, you jump in too!"

"Yea let's see some tits!" Timmy yelled. He began running around to get a better look.

"Get your ass over here, you little shit," Liz said and ran after her son.

Buddy threw a beer can at Chuck.

"You still want to go, asshole?" Chuck asked him.

"Anytime you feel strong, loser."

Everyone let's relax," Jarvis implored the crowed.

"Fuck you! You trying to fuck my wife," Chuck said.

"What's your problem?" Jarvis asked the man.

"Yea, I got a *big* fucking problem with you grabbing my wife's tits!" Chuck began making his way over to Jarvis, fists clenched. Then…there was movement from the woods.

"Bigfoot is back!" Louis began running over to the woods.

"There goes the Sasquatch hunter," Buddy declared.

Slowly, everyone began to separate and head back to their respective apartments.

Slymind Braintwist watched from a window and giggled.

Luckily, the rest of the night was uneventful.

***

"And the best means to an end, is when I turn friend on friend."

Brian Winters just wanted a mellow Saturday. His roommate, Kurt, never came home last night. Maybe he hooked up with the drunk again. Now, as he reached for the toilet paper, he found only a brown carboard roll. An empty roll! He'd kill Kurt. What a prick! Brian got up and searched the bathroom but there was no paper anywhere. He'd just bought a twelve pack three days ago. What the hell had Kurt done with it all?

At that moment the doorbell rang. He pulled up his jeans and ran for the door. A young, too-happy-looking man in a suit stood there. Never a good sign.

"Greetings and blessings. Do you know God?"

"Fuck you and fuck God, too!" He slammed the door on the man.

He was sweating. The AC was out. He washed his hands and grabbed one of the chocolate chip cookies he'd bought yesterday. But when he bit it…it was oatmeal-raisin! Brian hated oatmeal, he hated raisins more. He'd had a cookie yesterday and it had been chocolate chip. But now they were all oatmeal-raisin. Indeed, the label even said so. How was this? Had Kurt eaten them all and replaced it with these? Yes, that was it! He was going to give it to his roommate when he got back home.

***

Craig Floyd wanted to cry. He'd woken this morning and left his bedroom and somehow ended up in his kitchen. He tried to turn around, go back to his bedroom but it was gone. The kitchen was almost gone as well. The fridge sink and oven had vanished. He was trapped. The apartment had shrunken to nothing but a room only a little larger than a telephone booth. He blinked and was in the bathroom. But the shower and toilet were gone. Was this his end? Yes. The windows and door were also gone. He'd die here. Would they find him? He thought not. He figured the apartment would disappear altogether soon, and he would vanish with it.

He screamed.

***

Jarvis was getting back home from running some errands when he heard a commotion coming from the lobby. There by the mailboxes was a crowd, they were all trying to speak over one another. Everyone seemed to be holding a paper. Jarvis made his way over to the Horn family.

"What's all this?" he asked. Liz answered him by showing him a paper. Jarvis had assumed that everyone was holding Marlene's flyer. But the papers were a newsletter. *The Le Trou Du Cul Gazette.*

"I didn't realize we have our own newsletter here."

"We never did. But look at this?" Liz said, opening to a page in the middle of the paper.

"Corn Hole Game Ends in Violence!" The headline read.

There were even occupying photos of them all playing. One photo was of Buddy getting into Louis's face. Another showed Liz jumping on Bobbi. The last clearly showed Jarvis cupping Verna's breast.

"What the hell is this?" Jarvis said. "No one was taking pictures."

"Oh man, Jarvis. Chuck is looking for you, bro," Buddy said. "You sure got a good feel there, lover-boy! Look at you weighing that utter!"

"It's that goddamn Louis Green. He's always has a camera, searching for the Yeti and shit," shouted a man in the crowd.

"Bullshit!" It was Louis making his way over.

"Who else took all these photos?" A woman shrilled.

"I have no idea. But look here…I'm in half the pics. How did I take them?" Louis asked. He had his own newsletter, turned to a different article. It showed Louis grabbing the mobile from the woman at the lake. The headline read:

"Food Additive Scientist Sexually Assaults Woman in Broad Daylight!"

"This is bullshit! It's slander!" Louis said.

"Okay, this must be someone's idea of a joke," Jarvis said.

"It's awesome. My man, Jarvis, grabbing some ta-ta," Buddy said.

"Yea, what did them big, big titties feel like?" Timmy asked.

"Timmy, shut your mouth," Liz said.

Timmy began doing a little jig and shouting: "Titties! Ta-tas! Utters!" Liz reached for him, but the boy kept slipping her grasp.

"Get your ass over her, young man. Stay still."

"Jugs! Melons! Cans! What did them big, big titties feel like, Jarvis!"

"You want to know what my wife's titties feel like? Jarvis, get over here and face me like a man!" It was Chuck.

"Chuck, this is all bullshit," Jarvis said.

"It's right here in black and white!" Chuck said.

A fight broke out a few feet away. A black man was grabbing an older white guy.

"Is it you? You have it? Give it back!"

"I don't have nothing," the white man said.

"Says here you've been stealing shit," the black man said, looking at one of the articles. A few guys quickly broke them up.

While Chuck was distracted, Jarvis made his way out of there.

"Oh man. It's about time someone put out a paper like this," Buddy said.

***

Jarvis went up to his apartment. As he cooked dinner he read through the newsletter. It had to be a joke but who would want to see his neighbors fight like this? Many of the articles were about residents he did not know but all of it was nasty stuff. People fooling around behind their spouses' backs, a woman was named as the person who was removing other's clothes from the dryers before they were dry—in order to use the dryer herself— and the super (whose name was either Sanchez, Suarez or Santiago, according to the article) was fingered for sniffing panties, when doing maintenance in a number of apartments.

Jarvis ate in silence, looking again at the photo of his hand on Verna's chest. Someone was making trouble.

***

The little theater had about thirty seats. A third were empty. Jarvis sat in the front row. The Horn family entered and sat with him. Buddy sat close. He had a paper bag and put it down between his feet. He rifled through it and removed a beer.

"This is going to be boring as shit, you know," Buddy remarked.

"I hope not. I didn't think I'd see you here," Jarvis said.

"Shit. She made me come," Buddy pointed a thumb at Liz."

"Boring as shit," Timmy said, echoing his dad.

"Jesus, Buddy." Liz said.

"What, Babe? The kid knows this is going to be some artsy fartsy nonsense. See me, I don't like theater. I prefer TV."

"You really are determined to make sure our son ends up as dumb as you, aren't you?"

"Shit. You married me."

Jarvis saw Summer with a very good-looking man by her side. A too tan phony-looking asshole.

The lights dimmed. A narration began. The narration was Marlene herself.

"*Ladies and gentlemen. Welcome to an elegant evening with Marlene Davis, Veteran of stage, screen. You are about to witness the greatest comeback in arts history.*"

"Oh please," Buddy said. Jarvis could not help but laugh.

"Shut up!" Liz hissed.

A light lit up center stage. Marlene entered the spotlight. She was wearing even more makeup than usual, making her look like a corpse. She wore a long black robe.

"All of the men love me. I am the siren of stage. I am pure light. I've been through many hardships and so many have been jealous of me over the years. Oh, but I am strong."

Jarvis yawned. Buddy was right. This was going to be a long night.

Someone's cell phone rang. It was the guy with Summer.

"Yeah. No. I'm at some thing—"

Marlene glared in his direction.

"The use of phones, cameras or any recording devices is strictly prohibited!" She admonished.

"—look I gotta go. Okay later." The man ended his call. Summer looked embarrassed.

"As I was saying. I am a strong woman. Imagine, if you will, a time when I ruled the stage—"

A woman's voice cut through Marlene's monologue. Jarvis looked. It was Lula, who was standing and pointing. She was yelling at Kurt, who was two rows behind her.

"How are your balls feeling, Kurt?" Lula laughed.

"Sit down. You're drunk!" Kurt yelled.

"Come down here so I can kick your tiny nut-sack again!"

"Nut sack," Timmy repeated and laughed.

"If you cannot behave, you will be escorted from the theatre," Marlene said from the stage, even though there was no one to do the escorting.

"Tell that drunk bitch to leave me alone," Kurt said.

"Tell that hard-up shit he was lucky for the one night and to stop stalking me," Lula replied.

"*Stalking? Lucky?* Shit, I would not have touched you had I not been tipsy. You know about being tipsy, right you lush!"

"Both of you relax!" Louis Greene shouted.

"Shouldn't you be looking for Big Foot or aliens," Lula replied.

"Have another drink," Louis said.

"You fat fuck."

"Who are you calling a 'fat fuck', you slut?" Bobbi shouted.

"Silence!" Marlene said.

Brian Winters entered the theater and began looking for a seat. He spotted his roommate.

"You had better start looking for another apartment, you dick," Brian said.

"What the fuck now?" Kurt asked.

"You don't replace the TP! You steal my cookies!"

"Is everyone going fucking nuts?" Kurt asked.

"Just pack your shit and leave," Brian shouted.

"You got a bug up your ass?"

"Everyone sit!" Marlene shouted.

"I couldn't wipe my ass! My…my ass…my ass," he said and stuck his hand down his pants and began picking his butt.

"He's picking his ass!" Timmy said, excitedly.

"Maybe this ain't so bad, after all," Buddy said.

Brian began dancing around, digging at his bum.

"You're just pissed because I banged your sister. And I am going to bang her even better with this!" Kurt said, pulling at his belt buckle.

"What in holy hell," Brian said, pulling his hand out of his ass. He indeed had had a bug up his ass, as he held a giant fly in his hand. The unnatural thing flew from his grasp and commenced buzzing around the theater.

Kurt, his pants now down to his knees, looked crazed.

"I'm going to give it to your sister again, asshole! I wished for *this* last night and in the morning…."

He held his hardon in his hand like a weapon. His member was large…and black!

"You didn't have *that* last week, you shit," Lula shouted.

"I wished for a black man's dick and now I have one!" The cock stood in contrast to his pale white belly and thighs.

"Oh my God. He's got a gun," a woman screamed, mistaking his ebony penis for a pistol. A few people ran, yelling "Gun!"

"It's not a gun. It's a dick for crying out loud," Chuck yelled from the back. "A big black dick!"

"Hey, stop looking at it," a man yelled at his wife.

"It's huge," the wife replied.

"I wish I had a black man's dick, too!" The husband yelled.

"Me too. I want a black dick, too," another man screamed.

"Oh no you don't. I can't handle *that*," his wife replied.

"Me too," Timmy yelled out. "Who's giving out black dicks?"

"You shut up," Liz roared.

Someone from the back row shouted.

"Give it back! Give me back my dick!" A black man shouted. His pants were down, revealing a tiny white penis surrounded by a thatch of red hair. It was the black man who had grabbed the old man in the lobby earlier in the newsletter commotion.

"Now *that's* the limp shit that prick had when I had him," Lula slurred.

"No way. You ain't getting it back," Kurt yelled and ran from the theater, the black man on his tail.

"Look out!" Someone screamed, ducking the giant fly that Brian had pulled from his ass.

"That fly smells like shit! Don't let it land on me," a kid screamed.

"Everyone! You are in a theatre! Behave!" Marlene said from the stage.

"This is better than any damn play," Buddy shouted.

Merlene decided to trudge on.

"I have had to fight through life. From jealous peers, from obsessed suiters and even having to call the police on a bad boy who dumped the penny savers!

"You old hag!" Timmy said.

"Timmy!" Liz said. Marlene continued.

"He hid the penny savers!"

"I knew she was the one who told on me."

"I am woman. My vagina roars!" Marlene screamed.

The melee stopped for a moment, everyone looking at the stage.

"My vagina roars!" Marlene said and opened her robe. She was naked beneath. Her tits hung terribly low. Her pubic hair went from half-way down her thighs to her belly button.

"Oh Christ!" Buddy yelled.

"Put that damn robe back on!" Someone shouted.

"That's it," Liz said and got up. Timmy stared at the naked woman.

"Cover your eyes," Liz said.

"One step ahead of you, babe," Buddy said. He indeed was hiding his eyes.

"Not you. Timmy!"

Summer stood in the middle of the theatre.

"Brava! Brava!"

And the place cleared out.

***

Later, Chuck sat looking at the TV in confusion. The local news was airing the outside of their theatre. It showed the aftermath of Marlene's play. He'd been right there, and he had not seen any news crew or cameras. How was this being televised? What was going on? First the newsletter and now this. Something was happening here, he knew. Shit was going down, that was for sure. What kind of shit, he wondered.

***

So, it had been that old bag who'd snitched on him! He'd always known it but now the cat was out of the bag. Timmy fumed. And that was when the voice from the wall gave him an idea.

"That's brilliant!" Timmy said to the wall.

His parents had ordered Chinese food, after all the fuss at the play, and were waiting for delivery in the lobby. And he knew the old woman was still at the theatre, washing off all that make-up and, hopefully, putting on some clothes. Marlene never locked her door. Now was his only chance. But he had to move quickly.

He went into the bathroom and got the dirty business over with. He grabbed a plate and a sheet of foil. Then he quietly made his way into the bitch's apartment. He felt like he was being watched but Marlene was not here. His heart pounded. He moved his way quickly into her kitchen, found the refrigerator and placed the plate there. He was back in his apartment before his parents were back. This was going to be great!

***

It was the last thing Jarvis wanted to see. Well, maybe the second last thing. Considering a man had had his penis stolen, waking in the morning and finding your dick gone would likely be number one. However, finding Detective Black waiting for him was not a welcome sight. The cop was wearing the same suit and fedora as he has on their last encounter. He was eating a doughnut and sipping coffee. Again, Jarvis could not help thinking *bad movie cop*. The cup the detective was drinking from was plain white with the word COFFEE written on it.

"You again."

"Me again. Wow that must have been some show. Quite a mess out there."

"What can I do for you?"

"I don't know. Anything you care to tell me?"

"Not that I can think of."

"Well there was a lot of excitement out there. I also hear a friendly game of cornhole got out of hand as well," the detective said, holding up a copy of the *The Le Trou Du Cul Gazette.*

"And an argument over a game is something a detective needs to investigate?"

"Maybe. Maybe not. And you still have not seen anything strange here?"

"Not really."

"So, you don't think a kid stealing another man's prick is strange?"

"It's strange. But I don't see what it has to do with me. The last I checked, I still have the dick I was born with."

"Funny. Not so funny for the guy stuck with the little white prick."

"Well then you shouldn't you be looking for the prick thief, and get the prick returned to its rightful owner."

"I'm working on it."

"By following me? Also, I asked around and no one else has been questioned by you. "

"You asked around about me? I'm flattered."

"Don't be. What coffee shop did you get that from," Jarvis asked pointing to Black's coffee.

Black finished his doughnut and lit up a smoke. He scratched his head.

"You know it's the damnedest thing. I don't remember."

"You don't remember where you got the coffee from?"

"No. It was…just here," Black said. He appeared to be genuinely rattled.

He began walking away.

"Oh, and again—"

"Right. Don't leave town."

"I like you, Kyle Jarvis."

***

She finally got back to her apartment. She had moved them, of course. Marlene had stunned her audience. Art was to shock. Her comeback was underway. It would only be a matter of time before producers were calling again.

Her stomach grumbled. A successful night always made her ravenous. The play had not been a success per se. Those people did not know art. It was her mistake for attempting to bring some culture to this damn place. But they were *talking*. And that was always a good thing.

She headed to the kitchen to make something to eat. She needed to go shopping. She just seemed to not want to leave the Le Trou Du Cul at all lately. She really had nothing in the apartment. She put on coffee and opened the fridge. What was this? Leftovers? But leftovers of what? She had not cooked all week. She removed the plate from the fridge. She lifted the foil and screamed. A shit—a *human* shit was on the plate!

***

Sly felt himself growing stronger. The more he fired these people up, the stronger he'd continue to grow. It was all coming together. He wouldn't have to stay hidden in the dumbwaiter much longer. Heck was spreading here already. The woods surrounding Le Trou Du Cul, were growing, and with it all the mysterious creatures of Heck as its inhabitants. Mechanical fleas (as the name would suggest, these automatic insets did not need rest or substance, but existed only to itch and irritate) buzzed. A rock named Fredrick rolled around, attempting to trip people up. Leaves that looked like money flew here and there, tricking people into thinking they had found cash only to end up disappointed with a fist of fake bills, with Joey Buttafucco, rather than dead presidents' photos, gracing the useless tender.

Heck would soon emerge through the Asshole of the Universe, with he as it's king!

***

Marlene was removing her makeup and recovering from the vile joke, when she saw movement. Claudia's ghost stood in the living room.

"A shit show as always," the specter said.

"You…"

"Yup, me. You washed up old hag."

The ghost was young, the age Claudia had been when she had died.

"Get out!" Marlene said. "You're dead."

"I may be dead, but I am forever like this. Young. Beautiful. And I still act. They have theatres in the afterlife."

"Are you still sleeping your way through the ranks there as well, you whore?" Marlene asked the apparition.

"You're still jealous of me. Even in my death. How sad."

Claudia was tinted royal blue. The aura around her was a powder blue as well.

"You arrogant shit. Did you put that turd in my ice box?"

"No. But it was wonderful to watch you open it. I think I like that boy," Claudia said.

"Timmy! That little shit!"

"Leave that boy alone. He's got character."

"You would like that little prick."

"Look at you. You ancient creature."

"I moved my audience tonight. I am back to be the queen of the stage," Marlene said.

"You poor delusional relic. Look at you. Guilting your neighbors to watch your psychobabble on a stage in a bingo parlor. Pathetic."

"At least I'm alive," Marlene replied.

"*Alive*? Is that what you call this?"

"What's the afterlife like?"

"Judging by the look of you, you won't have long to find out. Christ you're old."

Marlene looked away. Looked back. Claudia was still here. Her face a beautiful indigo, her hair blueish-white.

"What's with all the blue?"

"Remember when I dated Pablo—"

"Yes, we all know! You're still bragging about that, even after death?"

"His blue period was my favorite. I live in the blue period, with my love, now."

The apples on Marlene's counter were blue now, as was her kitchen.

"Stop it! Stop making everything blue!"

At that moment Marlene could hear classical guitar playing, a nylon-stringed piece coming from her bathroom.

"What the hell is that?"

Claudia's ghost smiled.

Marlene opened the bathroom door to find an elderly man sitting against the tub, playing the music. The skinny man was in rags and hunched over the instrument, playing. Everything in the bathroom was a shade of blue, including the man. She recognized the scene as Picasso's *The Old Guitarist*.

"Claudia, get him out of here!"

But the painting/man played all night, keeping Marlene awake in the process. The only deviation from the guitar was Claudia laughing every so often.

FIVE

Buddy Horn - High School Super-Star

What the hell was that tapping? It had been going on for three nights now. A mouse? A rat! He'd had enough. Buddy put down his beer, grabbed a hammer and smashed in the sheet rock where the sound was coming from. He was going to smash the rat, as well.

Once he removed the sheet rock he saw an opening. A chain hung within the wall.

"What the hell are you doing? Are you drunk again?" Liz said, rubbing sleep from her eyes.

"There's something in here. A rat, I think. Or a bird."

"A *bird*? Are you fuckin' nuts? How would a bird be living in the wall?"

"I don't know, but look at this. It's a chain. What is this?" Buddy said, sticking his head in the hole. "What the… a little elevator. Holy shit! It's an elevator for midgets. This place must have been run by midgets back in the day. Cool!"

Liz looked into the hole.

"Wow. That may be the dumbest thing you have ever said. Which would then make it the dumbest thing that has *ever* been said."

"Oh, okay miss intellectual, what do you think a tiny elevator is for, if not for midgets? Tell me that, huh?"

"It's a dumbwaiter."

"Huh?"

"Jesus, Buddy. It's how people sent food from the kitchen to the rooms years ago. Considering how old this building is, it makes sense. Of course, there is not a kitchen on the ground floor anymore. It's just another apartment. So, since there is no use for it, I guess they covered it up."

"Why would anyone send food up in a midget elevator? That's stupid."

"I'm going back to bed."

Buddy stuck his head in the hole.

"I don't see any birds...or midgets."

"That's because no birds, or midgets, live in our walls. The chain must have been tapping against the wall. Now you will need to fix this mess."

Liz went back to bed. Buddy opened another beer. He went back to the TV. He watched the Spanish channel. He didn't understand a word and the silly gameshow had no subtitles, but the women were always hot, and hardly dressed, on the Spanish channel. Then the sound began. He turned to look, and the chain was moving. Slowly the dumbwaiter appeared where he'd made the opening. And somebody was in it. A little person.

"A fuckin' midget elevator. I knew it!"

But it was not a midget. It was...something else. He could not see it clearly yet. But a voice spoke. A high, cartoon voice.

"Hey, Buddy. It's an honor to meet such a famous football player."

As the dumbwaiter finished it's assent, the owner of the voice came into view.

"What the hell are you?"

"Is that any way to speak to the great demon, Slymind Braintwist?"

"Demon? You mean this midget elevator goes all the way down to Hell?" Buddy asked. However, this demon looked more like something created by Jim Henson than Hades. Indeed, he looked like a pink version of Cookie Monster with little devil horns. But while it was clear that the famous Muppet was cloth, this creature was clearly flesh and blood. Bone and fur.

"Well almost but not quite to Hell. In fact, Hell is overrated."

"Where else do demons come from?"

"I am from the territory just above Hell. A land called 'Heck'."

"*Heck*? You mean like Hell but called Heck?"

"Yes. I hope to get to Hell one day. I need to cause more trouble and earn my way in."

"That makes no sense."

"Think of Heck as Hell's farm team."

Buddy looked at his beer.

"Okay, I'm about nine Natty Lights in here. Maybe I'm dreaming."

"I'm not a dream. But I can help you with your dreams. You have a dream, no?"

"Uh, not really."

"No dreams? Mmmm. Maybe a place or *time* you wish to go back to?"

Buddy stopped as he was lifting the beer can to his lips.

"Did you say 'time'?"

"Oh yes. Tell me what you want, Buddy Horn. Let's see if Slymind Braintwist can't assist."

***

She was going to lose it. She'd moved to the sofa in the living room and still she heard Louis's snoring! He was spending too much time in the damn woods, looking for a fucking creature that surely was not there. He'd triggered his allergies and now sounded like an airplane taking off. He was sleeping soundly, and she was walking the floors. The selfish bastard. He'd accused her of trying to kill him with a LEGO and now he was keeping her awake. She got up and went into the kitchen. She saw pink around the edges of her vision. She grabbed the soup ladle from its hook.

***

Louis was dreaming of Bigfoot. He and the creature were listening to the old Andy Williams Christmas record. In his dream, the creature was not Ron Jeremy but the classic Neanderthal form so many videos and photos of the myth. Then he saw stars. He woke with a white flash of pain in his temple. And saw Bobbi leaving the bedroom. The soup ladle lay on the floor.

***

Jarvis Woke early. He'd had horrible nightmares all night. Dreamed that Maura's husband had found him. Since he was up, he decided to get to the laundry room early, get it all done. He was doing well in his new life. He'd joined a great support group. He was a recovering douchebag. The group used the same 12 Steps that people all over the world used to recover from everything from alcohol and drugs, to gambling and over eating.

"Hi, I'm Jarvis and I'm a douchebag," had been a very liberating moment. He just needed direction. He'd had so many lovers over the years, all ending badly-because of him. He'd had as many jobs over the years, as well: warehouse worker, electrician's apprentice, landscaper. And he'd been fired from every last one of them. But put him in a position to use a woman or lie his way into a someone's good graces and he was home. He could no longer sleep nights living that way. And he was enjoying the change. It wasn't easy, change never was. He was being tested daily.

He gathered up his laundry and made his way downstairs. He was looking around, assuring no one was waiting for him.

He heard a noise and froze.

"Hey, Jarvis."

It was Verna. Jarvis smiled nervously. Verna began putting cloths into a washer.

"Good morning," He said.

"Some play last night," Verna said.

"You ain't kidding."

"Did you see that big dick Kurt stole?"

"Uh…yea."

"These have to go in gentle wash," she said and held up a pair of purple, frilly panties.

"I'm not too sure how gentle these old washers are. They run a bit rough," he said, attempting not to look at the offered underwear.

"You like it rough? That it, Jarvis?"

Jesus, he thought.

"Where's Chuck?" He asked immediately and regretted the question. He knew Verna would interpret it incorrectly.

"Oh, he's bowling with his stupid buddies. He'll be at it for hours."

Jarvis turned to his washer and began tossing his clothes in.

"Oh. I have to put these in to," Verna said. She hiked up her skirt and pulled the panties she was wearing, down her thick legs. Jarvis went hard instantly. He'd not had sex in eight months. He considering making a move right here and now. It was clear she wanted him. His face flushed. But this was the last thing he needed. Chuck appeared to be a bit of a loose cannon and already thought Jarvis was after his wife. And he was doing so well with his recovery.

"I should get going."

"Really? Looks like you want to *come* rather than go," she said, looking at his bulge.

"Verna…if you weren't married…"

"You let me worry about that."

"Sorry, it doesn't work that way."

What was happening around here? People were fighting. The woods were closing in on them. And now this. Verna was not what most would consider a looker. She was older. She was chubby. But she was also sexy, very sexy. His hard-on ached.

"It's his own fault—Chuck has not touched me in nearly a year and a half. Just take me, Jarvis."

"Verna, it's not going to happen." He grabbed his basket and began to make his way out. Verna pulled one of her tits out.

He moved faster.

"Go on! You fuckin' faggot!"

***

He woke up with a hangover, a mustache and a mullet. Hot damn, it was 1988! He slipped on his acid washed Levi's and Chams' muscle shirt. The demon had done it! Now how did this work? Would time tick on going forward? Or could he stay here forever, live in 1988 forever? 1988, when *he* ruled! When he played football and when girls were nuts for him. When getting laid and partying was all there was. No bills. No worries. No wife and kid. And that's when he heard Liz's screaming.

"What the hell is this?!"

She ran into the bedroom, her hair crimped and teased to the ceiling. Giant neon loop earrings dangled from her ears. She was dressed in a pink neon top and stretch pants just at florid but the color of antifreeze.

"It's 1988, babe. And you get to sleep with the star—well a member—of the football team tonight."

"What the hell is going on? This can't be."

"Look." Buddy said, pointing to the living room. The flat screen that had been mounted to the wall was gone, replaced by a large bulky TV. The streaming box was now a VCR. The pastel paint of the living room had been replaced by dark faux wood paneling.

"How?"

"My friend, Sly, that's how."

"*Sly*?"

"Yes, Slymind Braintwist. He's a demon. But don't freak out; he's not from Hell. He's from Heck. It's not as bad as Hell."

"What?"

Buddy told her the story. How Sly gave him his dream. Liz almost passed out.

"Is this great or what?"

"Great? This is a nightmare!"

"Look at you. You're hot. Look at *me*. We get to do it all over again. The best years of our lives!"

"Best years of *your* life! And what about everything we've done? It's all just erased?"

"We get go to high school again—"

"Oh my God!" Liz screamed and ran into the hall. Buddy followed her.

"Babe, stop freaking. This is going to be great…"

He caught up with Liz. They were both looking into Timmy's room. It was abandoned. It was as if his son has never been here.

"You son of a bitch. You *selfish* son of a bitch!"

"Okay, Let's not overreact."

"*Overreact*! Are you fucking nuts? Timmy is dead!"

"No. He's not dead. He…uh…just hasn't been *born* yet."

"Don't use semantics with me, asshole!"

"Sym-ant-tic—"

"Word games! Dead. Not born. What's the difference?"

"It's simple. We just wait for the right time and we have sex. And bam, Timmy is back. And you call *me* 'dummy'?"

"You sorry sack of shit. So, we wait until 2007. Then we try and get the exact day we got pregnant. Then we pray that the exact same sperm fertilizes my exact same egg. You are a fucking idiot."

"You know what, babe. I don't like your tone."

"Oh, really?"

"Really. And the 1988 Buddy don't need to take this shit. I'm getting out of here." He flipped his mullet with his hand.

"And where exactly are you going?"

"To school, of course."

Buddy went back in the bedroom for his keys and wallet. He found them, but the keys were for the car he had in high school; the 1979 Pontiac Catalina, his very first car. His leather wallet was now his old Velcro wallet with the RUSH logo embroidered on it.

"Hell yes."

Then his eyes saw something in his closet. His gym short-shorts and his high school tank top. He stripped, admiring his young, slim body and got into his gym cloths. He grabbed the wallet and keys and left the apartment. Exiting to the sound of his wife crying.

***

Marlene was in the laundry room when the girl busted in.

"Marlene, I need help!" The colorfully dressed girl said.

"I'm sorry, do I know you?" The old woman asked.

"It's me, Liz."

"What..."

Marlene thought she was going nuts. It *was* Liz. But as a teenage girl.

Liz explained what had happened, but Marlene stopped listening after hearing 'dumbwaiter' and 'demon granting

Buddy his dream/wish'. That fucker, Slymind! Why hadn't he made *her* younger?

"A demon, you say?"

"Yes. A pink, fuzzy little demon."

"What? You are you talking crazy," Marlene said, trying not to show Liz that she knew exactly what she was talking about.

"Marlene, I'm eighteen years old again. How's what's happening here anything *but* crazy?"

Liz was right. This was all getting out of hand.

"And Buddy *conjured* this demon?"

"Buddy couldn't conjure an intelligent thought. The demon was in the damn dumbwaiter. Now Buddy went back to school."

"Dear, we don't have a dumbwaiter in this building," Marlene lied. She did not want anyone to know she'd met the demon or about the ghost in her apartment.

"It's been covered. Buddy broke thorough the sheet rock and freed it."

"I see. And then it gave him his wish to be back in high school?"

"Yes. But now I need to get Timmy back."

"Of course," Marlene said. But her thoughts were elsewhere.

They went to Liz's apartment for coffee and to think. Liz showed the old woman the hole in the wall. Marlene stuck her head in the hole. So, the demon had visited others. She thought of Claudia's ghost haunting her apartment, turning everything blue. As Marlene was looking in the hole, Liz let out a moan. Marlene turned to see the young Liz transforming. First her teased and frosted hair began going back to its old limp brown. Liz's hips expanded. Her florescent clothes morphed into the pajamas she'd wore to bed last night. Once Liz was back to normal, she ran to Timmy's room. But the boy was still gone.

"No!"

***

The excitement of being back in the old car waned when he got to the first stoplight and the car stalled. Buddy had forgotten that this car needed to be restarted at every light, every stop sign. Oddly, he'd forgotten this and had only remembered the good thigs about the car, the fun times he'd had in it. Like how the back seat had plenty of room for screwing. Memories worked that way. The halcyon years. But now that he thought of it, he couldn't remember actually ever having sex in the car. He got to the school and found a place to park.

Standing in front of the school, his heart beat quickly. By the look of the cars and the students' clothes, it was 1988 all right! He was jazzed to get in there, walk the halls a god again. But as he made his way into the school he felt he was getting strange looks. And he did not recognize any of the students.

No matter. He began making his way to the gym. A king to his kingdom. At the gym he was sure to see his old buddies. Maybe they would cut out. Go to Eddie's deli, where they were never proofed, and buy beer. They could invite some of the cheerleaders to hang out and drink and suck face. Hell yea!

But as he headed to the gym, he knew something was wrong. He felt something weird in his gut. The strange looks he was getting turned into downright stares. Some of the students even pointed at him. His stomach made a gurgling sound. He looked down to see his belly expanding back to its normal size. The tank top was now over his belly button, his hairy gut exposed. The orange shorts were riding up his ass like a thong.

He heard laughter. He looked up. The students no longer looked like something from the '80s. They were now modern, board and depressed-looking teenagers. Most of the students had their phones out and were filming him.

"Holy shit. His nut sack is hanging out!" Someone shouted, pointing to Buddy's shrinking shorts.

"Oh shit." Buddy cried.

And then an alarm went off. And he was tackled to the ground by two teachers.

"Hold him down. The police are on their way."

"Sly you bastard!" Buddy screamed. The students continued filming.

***

Of course, he'd waited until after sex before telling her that he needed his space and that they should take a break for a while. Summer could not believe it. What nerve! Jed was eleven years her junior and she knew it wouldn't last. But this was a shitty way to end it, even for Jed. She'd met him in yoga class last month and since then their relationship was little more than sexual. He'd assured her that his new-found desire to cool things off had nothing to do with another woman. What bullshit. And he then had the fucking nerve to excuse himself to take a shower. She now listened to the water running—Jed washing her sex smell off him. Her head throbbed.

Fists clenched, she looked into the hole in the wall, crying. And called to her angel for guidance. His little pink head appeared, his large googling eyes rolling.

"What do I do?" she cried.

His squeaky voice came from the darkness.

"The pain you feel will never pass, so make a sugar-daddy of his ass."

Summer went into the kitchen and put the double boiler on high heat. She began to liquify a two-pound-bag of organic, raw sugar.

***

He took the dumbwaiter down. And down. And down. All the way to Heck. He dreamed of the day that he would belong to Hell. Then he could *really* cause trouble. But for now, he would have to settle for raising heck. And he was doing a fine job of it here at Le Trou Du Cul. He had a lot going on. And now the hippie chick was going to give her boy-toy the shock of his life. The dumbwaiter stopped and Slymind got out. Heck was in cartoon for the most part. He walked along the strawberry soda river (it looked refreshing but if you tried to drink from it, however, you'd find the liquid contained a robust laxative that would render the drinker a month on the toilet in a painful and constant bowel movement) and stopped by a giant, green/yellow mushroom to inhale its narcotic vapor. He walked to the café to chat with his fellow demons. Purple Waters was here. He was about to turn around, but the pimp had spotted him.

"Sly, get your ass over here. Have a drink with your old pal, Purple," the high voice squeaked.

"Purple!" He faked enthusiasm.

Sly had slept with a few of Purple's girls recently (on credit). He also owed the pimp, as well as a number of others, gambling debts, and had been ducking out on the two-foot pimp ever since. Figures his first visit back into Heck in days and Purple is right here.

"I've been working over at the Asshole of the Universe. Been busy."

"Save it, fuzzy. You have my payment? Say no. Please say no, so Purple can fuck you up," the tiny creature said. Purple Waters may have been just two feet tall but was a badass. He was called Purple because he was so dark that he was almost purple. He wore a yellow zuit suit and matching hat.

"Would I skip out on you?" Sly said.

"Man, why don't you just get yourself a woman? Then you won't need my bitches," Purple said. "And then you would not have to get your ass beat by Purple."

But Sly was done with relationships. He'd been sleeping with a cute little demon for the last few months. But even though they had agreed that they were to be nothing other than DWB (demons with benefits) she'd began crowding him almost at once. It had been a nightmare shaking her. Even in the demon world, pussy was not without its headaches.

"I don't want a woman. Why bother when my man Purple here can keep me in 'tang?" Sly said, attempting to play it cool.

"You're not getting my money fast enough."

"Are you kidding? I have that place in a shamble. I'll get paid as soon as all them people kill each other."

Purple squinted at him.

"Well Purple needs his money," Purple said. He adjusted his hat on a jaunty angle, thinking. "Hey, Sly...you think yo man, Purple here could get up there and pimp them human bitches out?"

"Oh, sure. But I need to break them a bit more," Sly said. He didn't want Purple coming up to Le Trou Du Cul and getting in his way. He'd get paid soon and pay the pimp off. Be done with him.

"Well, just keep working on them. And then pay me."

"I will. Now, is Kraken-Girl available? I love them titties." Sly said. He liked her. She had the entire ocean in her hair.

"My man, take it from Purple, keep your dick in your fur for a while."

***

Jed showered off. He would finally be free of Summer. He enjoyed the sex, but it was time to move on. Summer had no money to speak of. He'd met a new woman in meditation class last week and while she was not hot like Summer, she was loaded!

As he was washing off the organic fair-trade African black soap, he heard the bathroom door creak open. Summer looking for another bang before goodbye. What the hell. But he was suddenly shocked when a wave of heat, like nothing he'd ever felt, washed over him. He screamed as Summer covered him in the liquefied sugar. As the sugar hit him, the cooler water from the shower hardened the mixture on his skin. It stiffened instantly.

"How do you like being a sugar daddy, you asshole!"

***

Liz picked up her cell phone. It was Buddy. He was at the 11th precinct. Arrested for indecent exposure. Exposing himself in a school, to students, to be exact. She had a good mind to leave him there. But his first question had been to ask if she was okay, back to normal and if Timmy was back.

Seeing Buddy in the holding cell with, what now looked like, a halter top and hot shorts, she would have laughed under different circumstances. She bailed Buddy out. A court date was made, and Buddy was going to be added to a neighborhood list of sex offenders.

***

Summer sat crying. Jed was a shit and deserved something for using her the way he had. But this? She had been lucky she hadn't maimed him. The sugar had crystalized on him, leaving him stiff and confused. He'd run out, screaming. He'd even left his clothes behind. What had gotten into her? Then she remembered. The celestial being, Sly. He'd clouded her mind. Slymind was no angel. He was making everyone crazy. This had to stop.

She had decided to go out for the day, get away from Le Trou Du Cul. But as she made her way to her car, a flood of things entered her mind: the stores would be crowded, traffic would be nuts, Jed may be out there waiting for her. It was almost as if some force was stopping her from leaving. In the parking lot, she tried but could not bring herself to get into her car. Then she heard glass breaking.

***

"So angry it makes you, when needed is one and still he takes two."

Louis had been driving around the parking lot for over twenty minutes. The AC had died in his tiny car and sweat was pouring off his corpulent body. Finally, he spotted an open spot. However, when he got closer he realized there was an emerald green Lexus (Chuck's car) parked in an obnoxious diagonal, taking two spots. He put his car in park, removed the crowbar from his trunk and proceeded to smash both head lights and all the windows.

***

Craig Floyd cried. The bathroom had shrunken more still, to standing room only. There was no way out. No door. No windows. He looked around for some way to break out of this nightmare. He noticed a hole in the bathroom wall, about where the toilet paper holder had been. The hole had not been there moments ago. It was perfectly round—as if someone held a paper coffee cup to the wall, traced around it and cut through the wall. He crouched as low as he could and yelled into the hole.

"Help! Hello?"

He heard movement from the other side. Thank God!

"Hello? Anyone there?"

More movement and then the person on the other side simply knocked, two quick raps, on the wall.

"Hello?" Craig said desperately.

Two fingers poked through the hole.

"Yes! In here!" Craig said. He was going to be saved after all! Then...

A mouth appeared in the hole, a bushy mustache and thick lips were all he could see. The guy on the other side was attempting to communicate.

"Yes, in here!"

The mouth made a wet sound.

"I'm stuck in here. Help!"

"Stick your dick in the hole." The mouth said.

"What? Help. I am trapped!"

"Put your dick in." And the mouth began making kissing sounds.

"Nooooo!" The old man cried.

***

Jarvis had jumped in and stopped Louis from completely destroying Chuck's Lexus. The crazed man held up the crowbar. He was drenched in sweat.

"How would you like some, dickless?"

"Louis, relax," Jarvis tried.

"Relax your ass, fuck stick!"

Louis hit the car once more and jumped back into his own car, drove away. Once Louis was gone, Summer came over to Jarvis. She'd been ducking behind her own car, hiding.

"Not that I wouldn't mind seeing you get your head bashed in but that was really stupid."

"What the hell is going on around here?"

"So, he *finally* notices. A negative energy is closing in here."

"I don't know about an energy, but something is happening."

"Yes. Perhaps the planets are lining up in a strange way or—"

"No, Summer. It's nothing like that. It's Carbon monoxide, or group psychosis."

"Yea right."

"I'm sorry. You're right, Summer. Some warlock or magical force is messing with everyone."

"God, you're an asshole. Can you prove that it's got nothing to do with the planets or a form of haunting?"

"You're asking me to disprove something that cannot be proven. Have you ever heard of the "'*Cosmic Teapot Theory*?'""

"What?" Summer asked and coughed.

"There was a philosopher, Bertrand Russell, and he used this as an analogy. Basically it goes like this: Imagine a man states that between the Earth and Mars there is a china teapot revolving about the sun in an elliptical orbit, also this teapot is too small to be revealed even by our most powerful telescopes. Now, because no one can disprove his assertion, it must be true. Understand? See, the burden of proof lies upon a person making unfalsifiable claims, rather than shifting the burden of *disproof* to others."

"Wow. First, why does it have the be *men* debating the universe? Secondly, you really just gave me a long-winded, circumlocutory, put down."

"I was just trying to explain—"

"When was the last time you left Le Trou Du Cul?" Summer asked.

"What does that have to do with anything?"

"When?"

"I can't remember exactly. A few days ago, I guess."

"But you're tried to leave since then and were not able to, right?"

Jarvis though about it.

"I...Well..."

"Have you ever heard of carbon monoxide poisoning making it impossible for people to leave an apartment complex?"

He *had* noticed lately that whenever he'd planned to leave his home, something entered his mind and stopped him from going. However, the choice was always his. Wasn't it?

"I could leave."

"Go ahead, then."

"What?"

"Leave. Show me."

Jarvis pulled his keys from his jeans and headed for his car. But the thought of bumping into someone he'd screwed over overwhelmed him. What if Maura's husband was waiting for him? He stopped. Summer smiled.

"Look, Jarvis, I don't like you and I know you don't like me. But you are the only person here, other than me, who seems somewhat sane anymore. Marlene is completely nuts. Buddy and Liz have their hands full with finding Timmy. Chuck and Verna are trying to kill one another. Louis and Bobbi are fighting now because of his obsession with Bigfoot. We need to work together."

"Okay, how?" Jarvis asked.

"We need to stop the demon."

"There are demons now? Are you kidding?"

"No. There is *one* demon here, Slymind Braintwist."

"What? Is this a joke?"

"I'm not the only one who has seen it. Look around you." She went into a coughing fit.

Summer grabbed his hand and began marching him around the grounds. She began pointing strange stuff out to him. But all he felt was her smooth cool hand in his.

"Look," She said, pointing to the lake. Bugs, that appeared from another planet, flew around the pink water. A green mist rose all over. Changes everywhere. There was something to what Summer was saying. Odd plants had also sprouted all over the grounds. The woods had become thicker and bizarre trees of all colors seemed to have appeared overnight. A green bird with a long thin beak flew over to the lake and pulled out a two-headed fish and gobbled it up in one gulp.

Jarvis rubbed his eyes. There was a humming sound along with a vibration. Jarvis and Summer looked up into the yellow sky to see a UFO. It looked exactly like something out of a sci-fi movie, a saucer.

"You have to be kidding me," Jarvis said.

The UFO buzzed around and was gone.

"So, you think we are both imagining the same thing?" Summer asked and coughed loudly.

"I'll make you a deal."

"Oh, I don't like the sounds of this. You men are all the same."

"Don't flatter yourself, Summer," Jarvis said with a smile. "You agree to take some real medicine for that cough and I will listen to everything you have to say."

She was touched he actually wanted to see her get better.

"Deal."

"Okay, tell me about this demon."

SIX

Heck On Earth

Jarvis listened to everything that Summer had told him about her encounter with the demon. She went back to her apartment only after he'd promised to help. There was clearly something happening here and whether or not he believed that a small pink demon was the cause or not, Timmy *was* missing. He was not sure how he could help but decided he was going to try. They had contacted everyone and were planning on a meeting later in the evening.

He walked around the alien landscape and saw a familiar figure in the distance. He made his was over to detective **Black**. Of course, the cop was dressed in the same suit and hat.

"Just the guy I was looking for."

"I have no doubt."

"I have reports of ghosts, monsters, UFOs, a man who was attacked in a shower, smashed cars, and a missing boy.

You still stand by your story that there's nothing strange going on here?"

"With all that on your plate I would think you wouldn't have time to pester me."

"Just doing my job."

"Shouldn't you be speaking with Buddy and Liz Horn and looking for Timmy? Why am I the only one around here who's ever heard of you?" Jarvis asked.

"Well I'm just gathering info. There's a method to my madness. And, as you said, I have a lot on my plate. You take care, Kyle. Oh, and—"

"—Don't leave town."

"Right." Detective **Black** turned to leave. He stopped and faced Jarvis.

"One more thing. Have you heard anything about a missing elderly man?"

"Sorry, no."

"Okay. Oh, I just remembered. What about time travel? Have you heard about anyone in **Le Trou Du Cul** going back in time?"

"Can't say that I have."

"Okay, you have a good day. Just one more thing..."

"You're a regular Colombo, aren't you?

"Colombo? What's that?" **Black** asked.

"The old TV show."

"Never heard of it."

"You're kidding?"

"Sorry."

"How about *NYPD Blue*?"

"What's that?"

"Another TV show."

"TV," detective **Black** said to himself. "Yeah, I think I've heard of that..."

"Of *Colombo* or *NYPD Blue*?"

"TV. I think I have heard of TV..."

"What? Detective **Black**, you never said what precinct you worked out of."

"I didn't?"

"No."

"You saw my badge."

"I didn't really look at it. May I see it again?"

The detective appeared to be in a daze.

"Uh, sure."

He opened his wallet and showed Jarvis the Badge. I was a white business card with the word 'COP' in bold black letters on it.

"That's not a badge."

"I…I have to go…"

And Detective **Black** left.

***

That night Jarvis sat in Le Trou Du Cul's meeting room. He was disappointed in the turnout. He'd asked all the residents to meet in the boardroom but there was only the Horns, Summer, Marlene and himself here now. He waited another fifteen minutes, but it was clear that no one else was coming. He was happy, however, that Chuck (and mostly) Verna were not here. Marlene was dressed in all blue, rather than her standard black.

Himself, Marlene, Summer, Liz and Buddy. It would have to do.

"I think you know why I have called you all here. There is a demon in Le Trou Du Cul and he's making life impossible for us all. We have to stop the fighting going on. Have to put an end to the transformations happening all over the grounds."

"And we need to get Timmy back," Liz said.

"Of course. That's the main thing," Jarvis said. He was embarrassed that he had not led with this. His douchebag tendencies coming out again. He was not used to leading. He was even less used to not thinking of his ass first and foremost.

"How do we get the demon?" Buddy asked. It was the most solemn anyone had ever seen the obnoxious man. Jarvis felt for him. *He's a fellow douchebag,* Jarvis thought.

"I know a few psychics," Summer said. She began going through her phone looking for numbers.

"Okay, that's a good idea, Summer," Jarvis said.

"Really? You are willing to consult a spiritualist rather than the cops?" Summer asked.

"I think we are past the cops here. Let's try this your way."

She smiled at him. Jarvis thought of how she'd held his hand earlier.

"Here's one." She looked up from her phone.

"Is he good?" Liz asked.

"Oh yea. He has a one hundred percent accuracy rate…but—"

"But what?" Buddy asked.

"Well, yes, he's good and is 100% right all the time. But he can only predict certain things."

"What things?" Jarvis asked.

"Um, like what color shoes someone will be wearing or if someone has a pencil rather than a pen in his or her pocket," Summer said, embarrassed.

"So, he can only predict useless information?" Liz asked.

"Yea, I guess so."

"How the hell is that supposed to help? This granola girl doesn't know shit!" Marlene said. Summer looked down.

"Marlene, name calling is not helpful. Guys, we are all under this demon's influence, but we have to try and not insult one another. Slymind is affecting us all. Last night Bobbi hit Louis in the head with a soup ladle because he was snoring. So, we need to understand that feelings of anger are not real, it's his influence. Summer keep trying," Jarvis said.

"Okay, Dear, I agree. We need to stop him before things go further," Marlene said. She still had not told anyone about the ghost in her blue apartment.

They all knew it was true. Le Trou Du Cul was shifting all around them. Inexplicable plants, and mushrooms, not of this earth, had begun sprouting up all over (including indoors). In fact, some of the mushrooms even had humanoid faces and would shout insults at those passing by. It had become apparent that Louis was correct: Sasquatch, as well as other creatures, lived in the surrounding woods. But rather than threaten their lives, these creatures did more benign, and annoying things—like stealing your laundry, or break into your apartment when you were out and stop up toilets with their huge bowel movements or eat smaller pets. Also, there was a sea creature in the lake (a man-made lake!) It was rumored that an otherworldly miniature pimp named Purple, was attempting to gather the women for a gaggle of whores. Worse still, they'd all come to realize for a fact that they could not leave Le Trou Du Cul. They were not locked in, but instead, found they simply could not leave—much like the characters of the Luis Burnell movie *The Exterminating Angel*. As a result, no one could do any food shopping and were left eating Louis's odd and failed foodstuff.

Summer had continued to get sick, even though she'd stopped drinking Sly's concoctions but had kept her end of the deal with Jarvis and took real medicine. She was feeling better now.

"We have to get Timmy back," Liz said and hugged Buddy.

"We will," Jarvis said with a confidence he did not feel.

"Anton Snow!" Summer said, looking up from her phone.

"Who?" Marlene asked.

"Anton Snow. He's a psychic. A friend of mine swears he cleared her of psychic energies that were giving her bad luck."

"Have you met him?" Marlene asked.

"Yes. Now, guys, I should warn you he's a little eccentric. He's very…colorful," Summer warned.

"Call him," Jarvis said.

"Jesus," Buddy moaned.

***

They called Anton Snow and explained the situation. He was willing to hold a séance the following evening. He said he would not charge them unless he was able to summon the demon and Jarvis thought this, at least, was a good sign.

They all said goodnight, promising to come together for the common cause of stopping Slymind Braintwist. Jarvis walked back from the meeting with Summer. They were silent for a while. Then Summer spoke:

"Thank you," she said.

"For what?" Jarvis asked.

"For convincing me to take the antibiotic. I still think you are a close-minded asshole, but you were right."

"And I still think you are a delusional tree hugger. But thank you, as well."

"For?

"For taking part in all this. You could have opted out like all the others. But you are here and helping. And you got us a psychic."

"Don't thank me until you meet him. He's a real character."

"More of a character than you?"

"Fuck you," she said with a little smile.

"Well he'll have to do. I really don't know what I am doing, here."

"Why are you so interested in helping the Horns?"

"We are all suffering here. And we need to help them get Timmy back."

"Yea but you are taking this personally. Why? You don't owe the Horns anything. This may get dangerous"

"Because I have been a selfish prick my entire life. And I can't stand to look at myself anymore. I'm sick of being so ugly."

They arrived at Summer's door.

"Let me ask you: if you can't stand yourself, who's the one doing the 'can't standing'?"

"I don't know. A part of me?"

"That's right. Your soul can't stand the things you have done. And I don't think you're ugly. I think you're actually kind of cute."

"Not as hot of that yoga dude you're seeing."

"Mmm…something tells me I won't be seeing him again."

"Yea, I'll bet."

Summer took his hand. God, she was beautiful. Jarvis kissed her. Her cool tongue darted into his mouth, rolled around his own tongue. He put his hand on her little waist and moaned as they kissed.

They made their way into her apartment. At once, Summer slipped out of her sundress. She wore no bra or underwear. Her little wiry body was tan and tight. He never wanted anyone more than he wanted Summer now; he'd never wanted *anything* more than he wanted Summer now.

"Summer, you are amazing."

"Come here," she purred.

He did. They never made it to the bedroom; they made love on the living room floor, Summer on top. She guided him in and moved on him like the most beautiful dancer. The nipples on her tiny breasts stood out firm. She smelled natural, like oils and sweat. Jarvis held on for dear life, trying not to come too quickly. But they jibbed exactly and finished together. Her dreads smelled of sandalwood as they danced across his chest and face. When they were done, they held each other. Jarvis hoped Summer was feeling what he was feeling. Hoped this was more than a one-night thing.

***

He'd figured it out. It was karma. He never believed in that shit but here it was. Payback was a bitch, as they said. But he'd only been a boy, about twelve-years-old. He'd had a hamster. A friend's hamster had had babies and he took one. His parents told him they could not afford a cage. So, he kept the hamster in a little cookie tin. The poor thing could hardly even turn around in the tin. Eventually the hamster had died. And now he was going to die the same brutal death.

"I deserve this," Craig said to the ever-shrinking bathroom.

Bright green mushrooms had sprouted around the dwindling bathroom. But at least the vile mouth was not in the hole now. He'd always hated faggots! Was this *his* Hell? To have a gay mouth asking for his dick through the wall? Craig Floyd was done fighting. He was ready to die. Eighty-two years was as full a life anyone had a right to expect. But he wondered how he would be found. Would the bathroom, and the apartment, go back to normal size upon his demise? He looked at the hole and noticed there was another, the same size. Then another. Before he knew it, there were at least a dozen holes in the walls. Glory holes!

"What is this? What do you want from me?" Craig cried.

He saw movement from the corner of his eye. The mouth again? To his horror, an erect penis poked out of one of the holes. Then another. And still another. Before he knew it, erections of all shapes, sizes and colors appeared to all sides of him. A huge green dick rubbed against his leg. A purple cock pushed at the side of his face. It *was* Hell (Well, Heck, but he didn't know that). Penance for the hamster and a life of homophobia. And again, the old man screamed.

***

Jarvis left Summer sleeping and made his way back to his apartment.

"Was the bitch good?"

A voice from the side of the woods. A tiny man appeared. He was dressed head to toe in yellow; a mustard color. He was so dark he appeared to have no face at all.

"What?" Jarvis asked.

"Purple is thinking of pimpin' that hippie bitch out."

"Say that again you little creep."

"Listen here, mutha fucka. Heck has come to Earth, bitch. I own the ass of every bitch here. Watch your step or I'll pimp out your ass too."

Jarvis made his way over to the little creature. The thing went into the woods. Jarvis followed a few feet but then heard a growl, smelled shit. He quickly made his way back to his apartment.

Out the window he saw the car. It belonged to Maura's husband. He'd been found.

SEVEN

A Dangerous Meeting

They waited in the meeting room and watched as a huge, white Cadillac, with gold rims, pulled up outside.

"He's here," Summer said.

"You have to be kidding," Marlene said.

A large man with a big pompadour of silver/white hair emerged from the Caddy. He wore a white and gold suit of shiny silk. Huge gold rings adorned every one of his chubby fingers.

"He looks like Boss Hog and Liberace had a baby," Buddy said.

"Buddy be good," Liz warned.

Summer did the introductions and Snow sat at the head of the table and gathered everyone around.

"Okay. Today we will be holding a séance to conjure the demon Slymind Braintwist," Snow said dramatically. "I can feel his hostile presence already. He's going to attempt to get us to turn on one another. We must be strong and resist fighting among ourselves during the séance."

"I thought you use a séance to contact the dead, not capturing demon?" Marlene said.

"Well I'm not a demonologist," Snow said.

"Well then it won't work."

"Do you have any better ideas?" Summer asked.

"Well I once played a medium in a play and—"

"No one gives a fuck about some rinky-dink community theatre when Abraham Lincoln was president." Liz shouted.

"I'll have you know you're speaking to a seasoned thespian."

"See? I told you she was gay," Buddy said.

"Buddy shut up!"

"What an ungrateful bitch," Marlene said.

"Zip it you old bag."

"Okay, I can't take these bad vibes," Summer complained.

"Guys. We need to do this together," Jarvis said.

"Jarvis is correct," Snow said.

"Just ask this relic to keep quiet," Liz said.

"You know what? I don't need this shit. Truth be told, that little brat never even liked me. He would throw dirt bombs at me when I was on the terrace, reading through lines. And he'd peep in on me when I showered."

"Reading lines for what, you old has-been," Liz said.

"And you told me to behave," Buddy said to his wife.

"*Has been*! You white trash bitch," Marlene said, getting up to leave.

"Are we doing this or not," Snow asked.

"Marlene, please sit. I really think we need to be vigilant not to turn on each other. This demon has gotten into all of our minds. We need each other to defeat him," Jarvis said.

"And what makes you the expert?" Summer asked Jarvis. He was hurt but knew this was the demon's doing. Summer turned to Snow. "He does not even accept holistic remedies and he wants me to believe he knows about trapping negative energies?"

"I never said I was an expert."

"He denies truth and worships at the altar of medicine."

"Why? Because I don't believe that warm water and lemon cures cancer? And medicine helped you!" Jarvis was getting angry.

"It totally does."

"If water and lemon killed cancer cells than what about people *without* cancer who drink it?"

"Huh?"

"People without cancer who drink lemon and honey in water or tea. Wouldn't it then be fucking them up?

"It has to be *organic* lemon—"

"Again, with this?" Marlene said.

"If you don't have an open mind—"

"Enough," Liz said.

"No! I've had it with your put downs, Kyle Jarvis You're an arrogant idiot," Summer said.

"You fucking tree hugger," Jarvis said. And stopped himself. Summer seemed to realize what was happening as well. She leaned in and whispered into Jarvis's ear. She smelled like heaven.

"Oh, my god. I'm sorry."

"Me too. It's Sly, not us speaking."

"Just tell *her* to not interfere," Liz said, pointing to Marlene.

"Me?"

"Yes, you. You got naked in front of my innocent little boy."

"*Innocent*? Please! The little bastard put one of his turds in my ice box!"

"Bullshit!" Liz cried.

Marlene turned to Snow.

"Look at how an actress is being treated? Can you imagine the world without the arts?"

"You're an artist my ass!" Liz said.

"Oh, and you and that boar of a husband of yours know about the arts!"

"Why are you bringing me into this? And I had to see you naked, too. I'm going to need therapy after that horror show," Buddy said.

"And why are you blue?" Liz asked. It was true. Marlene was tinted blue all over.

"Yea, Marlene what happened to you? You look like you should be in a coffin," Buddy said.

Again, Marlene got up to leave.

"People, please. Let's all sit and do this. We are giving the demon exactly what he wants," Snow implored.

Marlene sat back down. She did not share her own encounter with Slymind Braintwist, Claudia's ghost or her blue apartment with the rest, but that damn Jarvis was right. They needed to defeat the demon.

"Good," Snow said. "I am going to contact this demon and attempt to bind him. We are going to try and trap him." Anton Snow consulted an old book.

"And then what?" Marlene asked.

"I am not sure," Snow said.

"So, we are going to try and get him back into the midget elevator?" Buddy asked.

"The what?" Snow asked.

"Nothing. Please continue," Liz said.

Snow placed black candles around the area. He produced a piece of chalk and drew a sis-pointed star within a circle, placing dots within the circle.

"That's a Jewish star. What if the demon is not Jewish?" Buddy asked.

"It's a Seal of Solomon," Snow replied.

"I don't think the demon is Jewish—" Buddy began.

"Okay! Enough! Buddy get out. Sit in the hall until we're done here," Liz said.

"Are you kidding? I want to see the little bastard get back in the midget elevator. I hate the little bastard. And not because he's Jewish. I am not anti-Semite—"

"Out!"

"Son-of-a-bitch," Buddy said and headed out into the hall.

"Okay." Snow pulled a jar of water out of his bag and began sprinkling it around with his fingers.

"What's that?" Marlene asked.

"Holy water, of course."

"Oh, that won't do anything," Summer said.

"But holy water is always used in rituals," Snow said.

"Oh, Anton, don't you know anything? Holy water is nothing. You think because a priest waved his hands over it, that it's magic?"

"Well I don't know about *magic*, but…"

"It's just Catholic superstition," Summer said.

"It can't hurt," Marlene commented.

"Here, use this," Summer said, producing her own bottle of water from her purse.

"What's that?" Snow asked.

"It's *charged* water."

"What?" Liz asked.

"Charged water. I left it on my window sill on a New Moon. *This* is magic."

"Are you kidding?" Jarvis asked.

"Don't you start, Jarvis," Summer warned, smiling. Jarvis thought about them together. It had been great.

"Forget the water. Are we all ready?" Snow asked.

"Yes."

"Yes."

"Yes."

"Yea let's get the little pink prick," Buddy shouted from the hall. He was still listening.

"Buddy, Goddammit! Just go away," Liz yelled through the door.

"Sons of bitches," Buddy said.

Snow began. He read from his whorey book.

"Oh, hear the Infernal, and pink fuzzy names of Slymind, of Braintwist. From the depths of Heck. I conjure thee. Dagon, drink from my chalice."

Snow turned clockwise and pointed a stick at each of the people in the circle.

Summer grabbed Jarvis's hand. He thought this little act as conformation that their night together meant something to her as well.

"Call forth the Princes of Hell...I mean Heck, from the north."

The candles went out despite there being no breeze. Summer squealed. Jarvis put an arm around her.

Buddy could not just stand in the hall, dick in fist. This séance was nonsense. Anton Snow was full of shit; the guy only wanted their money. They would never get Timmy back this way. He pulled a beer from the six pack he'd left in the hall.

He went outside and began walking around. This place was starting to look like a goddaman fairyland. The grass was turning pink. The sky was a gold. The trees were all the colors of the rainbow.

"Daddy is coming to get you, son."

He took a long pull of her beer and belched.

He turned the corner and what he saw did not look remotely like Le Trou Du Cul. The place was morphing quickly now. The woods were taking over. Buddy was not looking at the courtyard (where he'd played corn hole so many times) but a world that looked like a run-down, ghetto version of Sesame Street. In fact, the famous sign was even here but read "Sodomy Street." There was even a garbage can that looked familiar.

Buddy picked up a rock and hit the can. The top opened and the creature he was expecting popped out.

"The fuck's the deal, asshole?"

"Oscar?" Buddy asked.

"You think you're funny, blockhead?" The thing in the can said.

"What? You're green. You're in the can."

"How would you like my green in *your* can? Balls deep?"

"What a mouth. You kiss your mother with that?" Buddy asked.

"No. I kiss *your* mother with this mouth, fuck-stick" The green thing said.

"You know what, Oscar—"

"My name ain't Oscar, chubs. I'm Pico."

"Pico the Grouch?"

"Pico the Prick," the creature said and lifted himself halfway out of the can to reveal a huge green penis.

"I'll be dipped in shit. God bless you, Pico!"

At that moment a mangy version of Snuffleupagus walked by. The creature stunk. As it got close to buddy, the thing farted out a huge shit as it passed, splattering Buddy's shoes.

"What the fuck! What's wrong with this place?"

"Ha! My boy shit your shoes!"

"I'm trying to get my boy back. Help me."

"Buzz off," Pico said.

A huge yellow bird flew by. Buddy looked up.

"Damn, in my world Big Bird doesn't fly. At least I don't think so."

A huge wad of sickly-looking shit flew from the bird's ass and crashed across Buddy.

"Oh baby!" Pico roared and begin pulling turds up from his can and pelting Buddy.

"Goddammit! Big Bird shit on me!"

Looking up, Buddy saw Big Bird fly away and a flying saucer further up in the air.

Buddy sat on the curb, head in hands. Pico stopped hitting him with his turds.

Look here, pal. Your son is not gone. Okay? If you lost your son in a spell, you are going to have to capture the demon who cast it."

"Some people are trying, but it's never going to work."

"What demon are you looking for?"

"Slymind Braintwist."

"That fucker?"

"You know him?"

"He owes me, and a lot others, gambling debts, booze, women," Pico said. Men were the same all over.

"Hello everybodyyyyyyy!"

"Holy shit, Grover?"

The lanky blue thing looked at Buddy.

"Wrong, fuck-face. I'm Chester. I'm Chester and I'm going to molest ya!"

"You damn demons are taking over. And you're fucking up my childhood memories," Buddy said.

"Yup. And I can molest you where you stand, dickless."

And then Buddy heard a familiar voice call to him.

***

Lula was walking around the complex, drinking a sausage pizza flavored wine cooler she had gotten from Louis, when she heard the voice.

"You will drink anything, you lush."

"What the fuck? Who said that?"

A large green mushroom laughed at her. It smiled a large floral grin.

"Come over here and give me head," the fungi said.

"You fucker." Lula made her ways over to the thing and hit it with the now empty bottle.

"Shit!"

She kicked it and the mushroom turned into a hundred pieces.

And then Purple came out from the woods.

"Damn, bitch. You a tough one. Purple got a place for you in his haram," Purple said.

"What the fuck are you supposed to be?" Lula asked.

"Oh sweetie, Purple is a pimp. I could work you for sure."

"Work me? You little shit!" Lula threw the bottle at Purple. Despite her intoxication, her aim was true, and she hit the tiny demon right in the head.

"Goddamn!"

Lula walked toward purple. The little pimp ran back into the woods. Lula followed but once she got a few feet in she came face-to-face with Bigfoot/Ron Jeremy. She got one look at the creature and ran.

***

Chuck sat in his recliner and put on the news. A pink animal sat at a desk. He was wearing a little suit like he was any other newscaster.

"Welcome to Le Trou Du Cul news. Tonight, we review Marlene Davis's one woman show. It sucked ass."

"Ha! It sure did," Chuck said to the TV.

"What's that," Verna said and came into the living room.

"This little pink fellow is giving the scoop here," Chuck said.

"Buddy and Liz Horn have not fucked in eight months," Sly said from the TV, in a mock news caster voice.

"Shit! This is great. I like this little guy," Chuck said, drinking his beer.

"And here's the video of Buddy Horn being arrested," Sly said and there was a quick clip of Buddy in tight fitting clothes, in handcuffs, being removed from a school locker-room.

"I'm loving this little pink dude. Damn, Buddy's fucking balls are hanging out," Chuck roared.

"And Chuck Wolfe strokes his willy to circle jerk porn when his wife, Verna, goes to sleep."

"What?" Chuck said, spraying beer all over.

"That's right, folks. Chuck flogs the dolphin, jerks the gherkin, pulls the pud, to college boys stroking vids. Let's go to the man himself to hear what he has to say."

"Chuck, what the fuck is this?" Verna said.

"I...I..."

"You watch that shit? From our computer?"

"I...of course not!"

At that moment the video switched to Chuck sitting in his recliner. The voice continued from the TV.

"Chuck, tell us about the gang wank videos you love so much?"

"What? Christ, Verna, turn it off! It's me! Turn it off. Now! Turn the fucking thing off!"

Verna was already at the TV but no matter how many times they attempted to turn it off, it would not power down. She unplugged the TV. But it stayed on.

"Help!"

They all heard the cartoon laugh in the darkness. Sly was here.

"Show yourself, demon," Snow demanded. A pink glow appeared in the corner of the room.

"Christ look at this line-up," Sly's voice laughed. "The fake actress, the pseudo-hippy, the dummies who parented the dumb boy, the cheat and this false psychic. What a gaggle of losers."

"And yet these losers have managed to conjure you, unclean spirit," Snow boomed.

"I'm here for the shit show," Sly said.

"A demon who can't even manage to belong to Hell. A demon who resided in the joke of Heck!"

"You fat faggot! I will trap you here too. This place has power."

"Oh, and are we supposed to believe Le Trou Du Cul is the portal to Hell?"

"Not quite. Le Trou Du Cul is, in fact, the Asshole of the Universe."

Sly appeared in the corner but he was translucent, like mist. They all went over to see him.

"Why have you summoned the great demon, Slymind Braintwist," the creature asked.

"Why? Because we want Timmy back," Liz said.

"Timmy?" Sly asked. He seemed confused.

"My son. The boy you took!"

"Oh. Of course. Well I will need something in return."

"What?" Snow asked.

"The troublemaker. Him," Sly said, pointing at Jarvis.

"Okay," Jarvis said.

"No!" It was Summer. But Jarvis was already walking toward the demon.

"You can have *me*. He's my son," Liz said.

"No. It's simple. I want the rabble-rouser. I want Kyle Jarvis. One for one, for the boy."

"Okay," Jarvis said again.

"No! That's not fair!" Summer said. "Why is Jarvis getting roped into it?" Her tanned face had gone white. Jarvis thought she was so beautiful that it actually hurt to look at her.

Snow leaned into Summer and Jarvis, he whispered.

"He wants you because you are powerful. He's afraid you," Snow said and rifled through his archaic book. He came to a drawing of a man in long robes, holding a staff. He looked like Jarvis.

"Is that you?" Summer whispered.

"Of course not," Jarvis replied.

"Yes, it is. You are the leader of the chosen. The sentinel," Snow said.

"No negotiations. Is it a deal or no?" Sly said.

"It's fine," Jarvis said.

And the door of the meeting room blasted open.

EIGHT

Buddy stood there with Timmy!

"Timmy!" Liz ran and scooped up her son.

"Lock the door. There's a mob out there. They know we are calling Sly, but they think we are in league with him," Buddy said.

"Buddy you found Timmy. How?" Liz asked.

"When we woke up in 1988, he was gone. But he came back when we went back to normal. When he saw all the crazy shit going on, he hid. The woods grew, and he got lost. I met Pico the Prick. He ran into Timmy and he told me where to look for him."

"Demon, you were tricking us. You never had the boy!" Snow said.

"Ah, you got me. But I am still free to run Le Trou Du Cul. And you can never leave."

"Just go away. Leave us alone. And get that damn ghost out of my apartment," Marlene said.

"Ghost?" Snow asked.

They all gathered close to the demon.

"We should kill it," Liz said.

"Yea, you're dead, you fuchsia fuzzy fuck," Buddy said.

"Wait, you don't want to do that," Sly said, smiling a rainbow.

"We've got you now, demon," Snow said.

"Snow! Are you stealing these people's money, like you took the money from that old couple who had lost their son?" Sly asked.

"What's he talking about," Summer asked.

"Ignore the demon. He lies. He's trying to get you to turn on me. Get *us* to turn on one another," Snow said.

"Or you, Summer. Who slept with her own sister's husband. You always had to one-up your older sibling."

"What?" Jarvis asked.

"That was before my spiritual awaking," Summer cried.

"Or your fearless leader. The man who's on the run from the man whose wife he's in love with," Sly said.

"What?!" Summer asked.

"Oh boy, this is getting good. Sly got all the shit on everyone," Buddy said.

"And Buddy, who likes to stick his finger up his ass when he whacks the weasel. Ain't that right, Buddy?"

"What?" Liz asked.

"Snow's right. Ignore the demon. Don't listen to him! Lies!" Buddy shouted.

"Oh, now you don't want to hear what he has to say? You like ass play, Buddy?" Marlene said, laughing.

"And, of course, Marlene. A real villain—"

"Shut up!" Marlene roared. She jumped for the pink entity, but her hands went right through him and he vanished.

"You shit, you lost him," Liz said.

Snow went back to his book; repeated the spell, but nothing happened. They had lost him.

"I'm sorry, he's gone" Snow said.

"You fake. You ripped off an old couple whose kid died!" Summer said.

"I knew he was a fake," Marlene said.

"And you. What did you do that you lost the demon to save your old ass?" Liz asked.

"I didn't do anything."

"Yeah right—"

The crowd outside began banging on the door.

"We have to stop fighting amongst ourselves. The people out there are pissed. We are going to have to let them in," Jarvis said.

"No," Marlene said.

"I'm with the old broad, they want to kill us," Buddy said.

The door was beginning to break down.

"Jarvis is right. The door won't hold forever," Summer said. She took Jarvis's hand.

"Why are they after us," Liz asked.

From the shouting coming from the other side of the door, it did appear the crowd thought those meeting inside were the one's responsible for all the trouble.

Jarvis headed for the door. Summer pulled him in close. She whispered in his ear. Her breath smelled like peppermint tea.

"I love you."

Jarvis opened the door.

"You cocksucker. You're fucking my wife!"

It was Maura's husband leading the pack. He held a bat. Maura was by his side. Once Jarvis had told her that they had no future, she'd told her husband everything. Maura wore an evil smile.

"You're wife too?" Chuck asked. "He's been trying to get in my wife's pants, too!"

"Bullshit!" Summer said.

"Verna, tell Chuck the truth," Jarvis pleaded.

"He tried to force himself on me in the laundry room," Verna said.

"Chuck, that's not true," Jarvis said.

"Are you calling my wife a liar, pretty boy?" Chuck asked.

There was a hue of blue to the side of the gang. A beautiful ghost appeared.

"And she murdered me," Claudia said, pointing to Marlene. A sad-looking man with a beer stein stood to her right, a cloaked woman holding a baby to her left. They were all blue. Picasso's *The Glass of Beer* and *Mother and Child,* respectively.

"Claudia, I'm sorry," Marlene cried.

"Murdered?" Liz asked.

"Yes. I did it."

"Maura, you should not be here. We can't leave this place. Why did you come here?" Jarvis asked. Summer came close to him.

"Are you sleeping with this ragamuffin? You have to be kidding me!" Maura said, glaring at Summer.

Her husband got angrier. He held the bat high.

"You can have him, sister. He's going to break your heart. That's what he does."

"Maura, why are you upset? I thought you said it was over with this loser," her husband roared.

"Go ahead and hit me," Jarvis said to the man. "I deserve it."

"I'll *kill* you, you prick!"

"Let's kill all of them," Chuck said.

"People! We have all been corrupted by the demon," Jarvis told the mob.

Sly appeared with the crowd.

"Not corrupted...*Enlighted.* This Kyle Jarvis has you all fooled. Marlene the murder. Summer the liar. Snow the charlatan, Buddy and Liz who birthed this evil child," Sly said.

"Evil?" Buddy said. "Timmy's a little prick, I'll give you that. But he ain't evil."

"Oh, says the man who was arrested for exposing himself in a high school locker room," Sly laughed.

"Don't listen to this demon," Snow said.

"I've been a selfish douchebag. But all this violence is not the answer. Haven't we all been douchebags? Isn't that why we are here? In this place? We all came here to redeem ourselves. As penance. We all came to the Asshole of the Universe," Jarvis said.

"Yes, this is the Asshole of the Universe," Snow said. "We have to fight this creature now. Don't let him turn neighbor on neighbor."

"It's true. He's clouded our minds. He's tricked me into fighting with my love. He's put Big Foot in the woods. UFOs in our skies. A creature in the lake. I've ignored my wife with my obsession," Louis said from the back. Bobbi hugged him.

"Kill them," Maura's husband said. The mob moved in.

"Stop!" It was detective Black. "I'll arrest the lot of you. Think about it. Do any of you actually remember moving here? Or do you just recall *ending up* here? Like me?"

The mob was quiet.

"The people who can leave, should get out of here now. Snow, Maura, you and your husband, get out of here before you can't leave," Jarvis said.

"Don't you tell me what to do!" The angry man said and brought the bat down on Jarvis. His aim was for Jarvis's head, but Jarvis saw the bat move and at the last second and avoided the head shot. But pain exploded as the bat came down on his left shoulder. Before anything more could happen, Detective Black pulled his gun.

"Okay, anyone who does not live here, it's time to leave."

Slowly, the crowd began to relax. Maura and her husband and few others left.

"Okay, now those of you who live here, are you *able* to leave?" Black asked.

One by one they tried. Once again, though there was nothing stopping them per se, they could not bring themselves to walk out the exit. Sly made his way to the front of the crowd. Like they could not leave, they also could not grab and choke the demon.

"This is my portal. My Gateway. My Asshole of the Universe. And you, Kyle Jarvis, are stopping me from getting Heck out into the rest of the Earth."

"So, it's true. Jarvis is—" Snow began.

"The sentinel. Yes," Sly finished.

"But…" Jarvis was at a loss.

"So, listen, Kyle Jarvis. You are the chosen one, the sentinel. So, here's the deal: you stop blocking me. And I will let you, and only you, leave. Deal?"

Summer looked at her feet.

"Not a fucking chance."

"Well then, you and I will sit vigil until one fails. I have eternity."

"I knew it!" Snow said. You are the chosen. The Douchebag 9."

"The what?" Buddy asked.

Snow read from his ancient text: "They will live in compound together. So be it. One will bring Heck on Earth and 9 will contain him. And the douchebag 9 will act as the gate."

"What the hell does that mean?" Buddy asked.

"It means that Jarvis, Summer, the Horn family, Louis and Bobbi, Chuck and Verna are the Cabal. Keeping the world safe but having to live in a Heck/Earth hybrid world. "

"The douchebag 9? What about me?" Marlene asked.

"You," Sly said, "You are not mine. You belong to Hell, not Heck. You are a murderer and not a douchebag."

At that moment a growl came from the woods. Purple Waters came running out of the woods.

"He's here. Satan himself!" The little pimp cried.

In the shadow of the woods stood a beast. Cloven hooves marched forward. They all shuddered. And Satan came forth from the shadow. But he was smaller than his shadow, thinner. Rather than hooves he actually wore Expensive Italian loafers. His suit was pressed and neat. His horns were bejeweled. Diamonds adorned his hands.

"Wow, I love his style," Snow said, smiling.

"Hello everybody," Satan said, is a soft, friendly voice.

"What Sly said is real? This is the Asshole of the Universe?" Buddy asked.

"Yes, sweetheart," Satan said.

"Is Le Trou Du Cul also the nexus of the universe?" Timmy asked. Liz moved in front of the boy.

"No. The nexus is, believe it or not, a microscopic teapot between Mars and Earth," Satan replied in a high lisp voice.

"Not a word," Jarvis said to Summer. She squeezed his hand.

"Holly shit, the Devil is gay!" Buddy said.

"Buddy Horn, *all* deities are gay. Don't you know anything?" Satan said.

"What? My god ain't no fag."

"*Your* god. Are you kidding? The guy with the white beard who rides on the cloud? He makes the rest of us look like Chuck Norris. Think of it, what straight guy wants to be a deity? All the jewelry, the gowns, the drama. But now let's get to why I am really here. Marlene Davis, if you'll come with me, please."

"What? No. You heard the pink Cookie Monster. I have to stay here," she said nervously.

"Nice try. But murderers come with me to Hell."

And Satan took Marlene and walked to the woods. Jarvis almost felt badly for the old, sad woman.

***

Later that night Jarvis sat by the lake with Summer. They watched the creature come up to eat the mixed berry and cauliflower muffins they threw in the lake.

"Do you love that Maura woman?" Summer asked.

"No. I cared about her after a while, but it was nothing," Jarvis said, rubbing his sore shoulder.

"Are we together, for real? Are we even capable of that, two douchebags like you and I?" Summer asked.

"Yes. I think we are."

"Do you love me?"

"Absolutely. I adore you."

"I love you, Kyle."

"How sweet…"

At first, they thought it was one of the speaking mushrooms taunting them. But it was Detective Black. He had a glass and a bottle of whisky. In fact, the bottle simply said "WHISKY" on it. He looked drunk and sick.

"Detective," Jarvis said. "Are you okay?"

"Sure…maybe…not really. I am nothing but a bad movie cop, just as you said, Jarvis. And I think I know why."

"Why?"

"I'm not real. I don't know how…I don't know why. But I just am. You guys live well. Keep Heck contained. It's time for me to go"

"Go where?" Jarvis asked.

"I'll let you know when I get there. Have a drink." He handed the bottle over. Jarvis accepted it and took a swig. It tasted like nothing. Stage whisky, Marlene would have called it. But Black was clearly drunk from the stuff.

Black walked into the wood and disappeared. Never to be seen again.

EPILOGUE

It was difficult as first but the douchebag 9 all learned to live in their new world as best they could. Verna came clean that Jarvis had never tried to rape her, and Chuck eventually mellowed. There were others who were not of the 9 who actually *chose* to stay. William LeBron, the black man who had lost his dick, decided to stay in hopes of getting his member back and get rid of the tiny white prick he was stuck with.

Kurt could not go back to his apartment and Chuck and Verna had taken him in. His new penis was satisfying Verna, and Chuck said he was happier than ever just watching and being a cuckold, whatever that exactly meant.

Louis and Bobbi created a Public Access (or *pubic* access, as Buddy calked it) show about Bigfoot, and the other creatures in the woods and it became a huge success—in fact, there were rumors that they may even get picked up by a major network. It had turned out that sasquatch found Louis' mustard pudding irresistible and Louis was able to capture the creature with the dessert.

Since they could not leave, Buddy started an actual corn hole league and became the commissioner. Liz was happy that, for once, her husband was not living in the past. Buddy's new friend, Pico The Prick, had taught Timmy some tricks. One such trick was how to spy on all of the women in the complex while they showered. The little bastard was out most days now, rather than sitting on his ass playing video games and his parents were happy with that at least.

***

Marlene hated Hell and she supposed that was the whole point. She was to constantly put on plays in the hot muggy theater, where she was condemned to forever mess up her lines, no matter how much she studied them.

EPILOGUE TWO
(Is there such a thing?)

The attic was like a sauna. But she'd promised herself that she was going to clean out the place today and was doing a good job of it until she stopped to look at the box. The label on the box said: "school stuff.' She expected to open it and find a bunch of drawings, essays and such. But the box only contained one item. A diorama she'd created in 1978. She'd gotten an "A" in art for it, she recalled. She could remember making this back when she and her parents had lived in that insane apartment complex. The place where all the weirdness had happened. She could remember her teacher asking who all the people represented and she could not be sure. They were just modeled after people she'd seen around the neighborhood, or in stores. A fat man and his plain-looking wife, a young white woman with her hair done like a Rasta. She had created and painted all the figures first and then built the diorama, which was based on an apartment complex. It was a mashup, really. And she could also recall...the demon. A chubby, pink thing about two feet tall with goggling eyes. She'd convinced herself in the years following the incident and her family moving from the crazy place, that it never really happened. Fuzzy monsters? Trees that grew money? Impossible.

She remembered now the demon had possessed the diorama (along with a number of other toys). While she had never actually seen the figures move, they would constantly end up in different places and positions within the diorama. One time she even found the white Rasta sitting on the lap of a male figure, in a dirty way. But now she remembered why she saved it in a box. Why she kept it safe. They were all alive! Then she noticed a figure that didn't belong, one of her brother's old action figures. A cop-looking figure. That must have been in the storage box and fell into the diorama. The action figure was from an old '70s TV show called *The Midnight Stalker*. He was Detective Nick Black, a cop with a knack for stopping supernatural criminals. He didn't belong here. She removed the figure from the diorama now.

More than ever she wanted to get rid of the diorama, but just knew the figures within were alive, somehow. She did not know what place or even what *time* they existed in, but she knew they lived. The demon had done that. If she smashed it or threw it away would they all die? Were they aware that they were figures in a kid's diorama, or did they actually believe they lived? Had Sly supplied them with pasts and purpose? Maybe she even lived in another person's diorama…or story. How many things had Slymind Braintwist possessed over the years? She would continue to keep the diorama safe.

What else could she do?

About The Author

Sal Cangemi writes books, which, considering where you're reading this, you already know. He is best known for writing absurdist satires that flirt with horror and black comedy without ever committing to either *genre.*

His plays, *Avenue L* and *In the Kotten Kandy Lounge* were staged, but he chooses to concentrate on novels and novellas these days.

When not writing, Sal can be found enjoying a good cigar, watching movies (that most people have never heard of), and, of course, reading.

He lives in New York with his wife, daughter, and cats.

Other HellBound Books Titles
Available at: www.hellboundbookspublishing.com

The Anthology of Bizarro

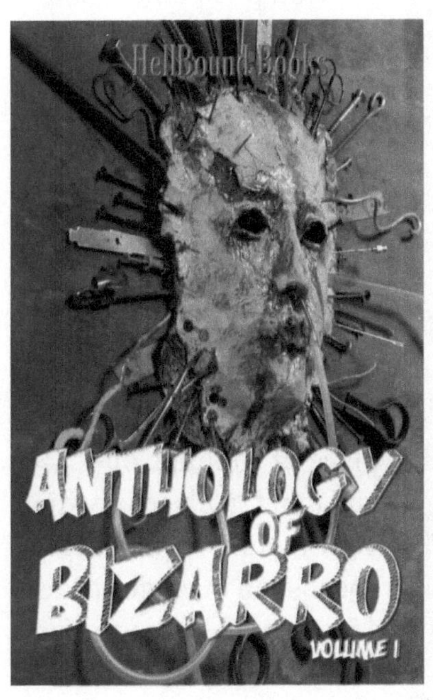

Welcome to the wonderfully horrific world of Bizarro - that dark, forbidding corner of the horror genre where absolutely anything goes and one may delve into the farthest recesses of the authors' warped imaginations.

Prepare yourself, dear reader, for a journey into the unknown reaches of terror, from which you can only hope you will return with your sanity intact...

Enjoy 16 outstanding stories from:

Scott McGregor, A.L. King, Garvan Giltinan, Keith Kennedy, Robert Prescott, T.M. Morgan, Lee Rozelle, John W. Leonard, A.L. King, Matthew McKiernan, Aron Beauregard, Ken Goldman, Victor Marrow, Ryan Woods, and Stephen Daultrey

The Toilet Zone
RESTROOM READING AT ITS MOST FRIGHTENING!

Compiled and edited by the grand master of 80's schlock horror, Bret McCormick, each one of this collection of 32 terrifying tales is just the perfect length for a visit to the smallest room....

At the very boundaries of human imagination dwells one single, solitary place of solitude, of peace and quiet, a place in which your regular human being spends, on average, 10 to 15 minutes - at least once every single day of their lives.

Now, consider a typical, everyday reading speed of 200 to 250 words per minute - that means your average visitor has the time to read between 2,500 to 4,000 words, which makes each and every one of these 32 tales of terror - from some of the best contemporary independent authors - within this anthology of horror the perfect, meticulously calculated length. Dare you take a walk to the small room from where inky shadows creep out to smother the light and solitude's siren call beckons you?

Dare you take a quiet, lonely walk into… The Toilet Zone

Schlock! Horror!

An anthology of short stories based upon/inspired by and in loving homage to all of those great gorefest movies and books of the 1980's (not necessarily base in that era, although some do ride that wave of nostalgia!), the golden age when horror well and truly came kicking, screaming and spraying blood, gore & body parts out from the shadows...

This exemplary 80's themed/inspired tales of terror has been adjudicated and compiled by one Mr Bret McCormick, himself a writer, producer and director of many a schlock classic, including *Bio-Tech Warrior*, *Time Tracers*, *The Abomination*, *Ozone: The Attack of the Redneck Mutants* and the inimitable *Repligator*.

Featuring stories from: Todd Sullivan, Timothy C Hobbs, Mark Thomas, Andrew Post, James B. Pepe, Thomas Vaughn, Edward Karpp, Jaap Boekestein, Lisa Alfano, L. C. Holt, John Adam Gosham, Brandon Cracraft, M. Earl Smith, Sarah Cannavo, James Gardner, Bret McCormick, and James H. Longmore.

Puckered

Percy is kinky.
Percy is perverted.
Percy is a loner.
Percy is sneaky…

…but most of all, Percy wants to be left alone.

Whether it be a nagging mother or something from his past, it feels like he is always trying to escape something.

Will he be able to find his own peace, or will the real world catch up to him?

There will be blood.
There will be s**t.
There will be unusual sexual kinks.
But most of all, there will be murder…

An Unholy Trinity Volume 2

FOUR HORRIFYING NOVELLAS,
FOUR EXCEPTIONAL AUTHORS,
ALL IN ONE PHENOMENAL BOOK!

THE BLOODMOON EXPRESS - M.R. Wallace

Following a failed case in London three years before, Ian DeWitt finds himself on Le Train Bleu. The famous passenger train will ferry him to the warm shores of the Mediterranean for a much-needed rest. Ian soon finds that the horrors of the past have followed him, and the resplendent luxury train becomes the hunting ground for a monster all too familiar to the beleaguered Scotland Yard detective. Running out of time and woefully unequipped to combat such a beast, DeWitt must discover the identity of the creature and attempt to stop it before they are torn to shreds.

SAVAGES FOR REVENGE - Alex Marroquin

Failing as an artist, Derrick de Sousa travels to Argentina to recover his artistic inspiration after his college sweetheart invites him to reunite with her at Buenos Aires. Instead, he finds himself forced into a path of murder and cannibalism by a madman convinced that all humans must die in order to preserve the natural world for himself.

This mysterious killer, armed to the teeth for his 'war against humanity,' forces Derrick to follow in his bloody footsteps across

Argentina. But with each life he takes, Derrick finds it harder to drop the weapon in his hand.

GARVEY'S EATS - Kenneth Seward
Deep in the backwoods of Texas sits a diner named Garvy's Eats, famous for its burger, the Garvy Special. Whitney and Tegan, best friends since Jr. High, are on a road trip to Mexico before college starts in the fall. After a thunderstorm forces the friends to take a detour, they end up at the diner where Roy Garvy wants the two girls for meat on the Garvy Special. Now with a monstrous, sick and twisted man known only as the Hellbilly hunting them down, the two girls must fight for their lives or risk ending up being served on a bun with a side of fries.

BONUS NOVELLA: MILK TEETH – Wren Pasdot

**A HellBound Books LLC
Publication**

http://www.hellboundbookspublishing.com

Printed in the United States of America